FIRE
IN THE
BOSQUE

FIRE
IN THE
BOSQUE

BARBARA SPENCER FOSTER

SANTA FE

Cover art by Frances Autry Jones

Sunstone books may be purchased for educational, business, or sales promotional use. For information please write: Special Markets Department, Sunstone Press, P.O. Box 2321, Santa Fe, New Mexico 87504-2321.

Library of Congress Cataloging-in-Publication Data:

Foster, Barbara Spencer, 1927-
Fire in the bosque / by Barbara Spencer Foster.
p. cm.
ISBN 0-86534-433-7 (pbk. : alk. paper)
1. Ranch life—New Mexico—Fiction. I. Title.

PS3556.O7575F57 2006
813'.6—dc22

2005032793

Published in

WWW.SUNSTONEPRESS.COM
SUNSTONE PRESS / POST OFFICE BOX 2321 / SANTA FE, NM 87504-2321 /USA
(505) 988-4418 / ORDERS ONLY (800) 243-5644 / FAX (505) 988-1025

Dedicated to my loving and loyal little sister,

Verna Nell Spencer Whitehead

1

~~~~~~

RENA TURNED OFF HER COMPUTER and got up from her desk with a relieved sigh. She looked out the window that faced Lomas Street and stretched her arms high above her head. As she lowered her hands slowly down, the southwestern sun sent glittery sparks dancing on the white walls from the rings on her fingers. She looked at her diamonds for a moment and then roughly grabbed her left hand. She yanked the rings off and violently threw them against the wall as an explosive "Damn!" escaped her lips.

The woman's shoulders shook, and her long burnished hair fell across her hands as her head drooped, and she slowly raised trembling fingers to her brow.

"Dear God, what am I going to do?" she whispered hoarsely. "Help me, Lord. My life is such a mess."

At that moment the phone rang shrilly and brought her back to reality. She wearily pushed her hair back and quickly swiped a hand across her eyes. She waited until the third ring before she answered, hoping her voice wouldn't betray the emotion she was feeling. "Rena Brooks' office. May I help you?"

"You surely can, Ms. Brooks," came the cheery answer. Then the voice continued in a slightly concerned tone, "But am I calling at a bad time?"

Rena recognized the confident voice of Adam Harrington, Chief of Staff at the hospital. She quickly collected her thoughts. "Not at all," she said in an assuring tone.

"Good," he said. "I have something I want to show you for your approval this evening. I hope we can have dinner."

Rena knew what Adam wanted to show her. And a week ago it was the thing she had thought she wanted most in the world. Now, for some reason, she wasn't so sure.

"Adam, I'm going up to check on Mother. Let me call you back later?"

"Sure thing." It was Adam's turn to pause. "Don't be long. I think you're going to like what I've found."

"I'll get back to you," Rena said briskly and placed the phone back in its cradle. She then turned and walked slowly to the window as her thoughts spun chaotically through her head. He wants me to look at an apartment where we can steal away for romantic trysts. It will be a place hidden away so his socialite wife can never find us, she told herself. "And I dreamed of something like this happening. Now I'm not so sure. What's wrong with me?" she whispered aloud.

The rings lay on the carpet where they had fallen after hitting the wall. Slowly she bent down to retrieve them. Holding them in her palm as she gazed at them reflectively, she murmured, "So beautiful and so expensive, but so meaningless. Why don't you come home, Taylor? Why can't Washington get along without you?"

Rena dropped the rings in her desk drawer and closed it with finality. "I think I know," she declared vehemently. "You have other interests."

Rena's high heels clicked sharply in time to her thoughts as she walked to the elevator and pushed the number for her mother's hospital floor. As she got off and headed down the long corridor, visions of the two men in her life whirled through her head. Taylor: the shy young college student, the flustered groom, the workaholic husband, the man who seemed absent from her even when he was with her. And Adam: the handsome successful surgeon, the charming escort, the romantic lover, the man who would give her anything except a wedding ring.

"Mother, if you only knew," she said under her breath as she entered the depressing hospital room.

The woman in the narrow bed didn't acknowledge her visitor although she must have heard her footsteps.

"Hello Mother." Rena tried to sound upbeat.

"What are you mumbling about?" her mother asked, her eyes remaining closed.

"I was thinking about today being your last treatment," Rena said brightly.

The old woman's eyes opened wide. "That's right," she said in a stronger voice. "And I'm not going to that half-way house they want to put me in." Her blue eyes had almost as much fire in them as the diamonds Rena had just put away. "Do you hear me, Lorena? I'm not going there." The eyes closed again with finality.

Earlier in the day, the social worker at the hospital had told Rena that the doctors were suggesting her mother be put in their facility for outgoing patients where she could receive post medical care and therapy before being totally dismissed. Her chemo treatments were concluded for a time, but she needed monitoring and therapy treatments for two weeks.

"Mother," Rena said softly, "Your doctors say you have responded well to your treatments. They just want to watch you for a short time before you go home. You know, you have to be as cooperative as possible. It will only help your chances for complete recovery."

The blue eyes in the weathered face opened again and stared up at the ceiling. "Listen to me, Lorena," she said in a firm voice. "It doesn't matter what I do or what my doctors do. I'm not going to beat this cancer, but that's not important now. I'm ready to go to my people. I'm lonely here without them. But before that happens I don't want to stay in any kind of a hospital any longer." Turning her gaze to her daughter she pleaded, "I just want to go home. Let me die at home in my own bed."

"You can't stay home alone, Mother."

"I know that."

"Well, what are we going to do?"

The expressionless blue eyes shifted to Rena's face and held firmly.

To escape this unyielding gaze, Rena turned and walked over to the window and looked out on the pitched rooftops that covered this huge hospital facility. She wants to go home to the ranch at Socorro, she thought. But my brother's wife can't take care of her. She's got two little ones and another on the way. I'd have to hire someone to be with her. Good help doesn't come easy. What am I going to do?

"Let me think about it, Mother," she said softly. "I'll see what I can figure out."

"You're a good girl," was her mother's faint reply.

Back in her office, Rena collapsed into a chair. She put her head down on her arms as the tears came. She didn't know whether she was crying for her mother or for herself.

Her mother's words kept running through her mind. "You're a good girl, you're a good girl, you're . . . "

"She said I'm a good girl!" Rena marveled. "She never gives me compliments. Her compliments were always for my brother. Everything he did was great; nothing I did ever warranted her attention."

Rena's thoughts went back to her lonely childhood. She knew her father loved her, and her happiest times were when she rode beside him on her little pony while she looked up at him on his big red thoroughbred. But he didn't often have time away from his ranch chores to pay attention to his little girl.

The lonely child had loved going to school because she had become very close to some of her teachers. She worked hard to make good grades, but her mother barely glanced at her straight "A" report cards. Her father, on the other hand, bragged about his smart little girl and always told her how pretty she was, while her mother pushed her away and had eyes and arms only for Boone, the little boy who was the center of her life.

Rena had grown accustomed to being ignored by her mother. That's just the way things were in her life. And after her father died as the result of his horse falling on him when she was in college, Rena went her lonely but self-sufficient way.

Rudy Steiner had made arrangements for his daughter to go to the Albuquerque Business School after her high school graduation. She had come home from classes over a holiday and met Taylor Brooks who was attending the engineering college in Socorro. Taylor was a quiet, serious young man who had definite goals set for his life. Young marriage was not in the plan. But he found the pretty ranch girl too hard to resist, and the two were married when Rena finished her business course. She returned to

Socorro and got a job at the college in the business office, and Taylor continued school until he got his degree.

Rena was sure she had married the most wonderful man in the world, and she no longer felt so alone now that she had someone who loved only her.

When Taylor graduated with an electrical engineering degree, he got a job at Sandia Base in Albuquerque. Rena found an office job, and the young couple bought a modest home near Kirtland Air Force Base. Rena was happy with her new life in the big city, and she went home to Socorro only occasionally. Her mother didn't seem to miss her very much. Her brother took over the ranch when he finished high school, and he ran it to his mother's satisfaction. When he married a local girl, she built a house for the young couple close to the family home.

Time went on, and Taylor's hard work paid off when he was promoted to the administrative level. Rena got a better job in the University Hospital, and they bought a nicer home in the foothills of the Sandia Mountains on the east outskirts of town. Everything was going right for Mr. and Mrs. Taylor Brooks, but the years had taken the zest out of their marriage. Taylor worked longer hours and traveled out of town frequently. When he was home, he seemed tired and moody. Rena grew accustomed to his silence just as she had accepted her mother's disinterest in her life.

Rena had filled in the lonely hours when Taylor was gone by decorating the house and working in her yard. She made an attractive southwestern style cactus garden and had a large guitar shaped birdbath built to lure in the desert birds. She remembered the pathetic yard back in Socorro where the lizards and horned toads ran around the few hardy flowers her mother attempted to grow in the sandy yard. Her attractive yard afforded her much satisfaction.

The lonely young housewife and career girl soon developed friendships with some of the other girls who worked in the hospital. Sometimes after work they went to a show at the Kimo Theater or had a light drink at the Night Owl Bar. She even bought a season ticket for the performances at Pope Hall. "I'll try to give myself some culture," she had laughingly told Taylor. Maybe you'll find me more interesting, she had thought to herself.

Rena knew her long, naturally wavy blonde hair and curvy figure received its share of admiring glances when she was out with the girls. And although she enjoyed flirting and having a good time, she never responded to any of the propositions she received. Her strict Lutheran upbringing reminded her she must be true to her husband.

However, that had all changed the night of the hospital Christmas party a year ago when she caught the eye of the chief of staff, Dr. Adam Harrington. His wife was home ill, and he had come to the party alone. When he asked Rena to dance, she felt she was moving on magic air as he held her in his strong arms and whirled her gracefully around the room. He was attentive to her all evening, and when he asked to see her again as they swayed slowly to the last waltz, she couldn't refuse.

Rena was putty in the handsome doctor's hands. Soon after that, they had spent a weekend skiing in Angel Fire, a resort north of Taos, and all the love she had craved for a lifetime was hers in his arms. The fact that he was married and had a family made no difference to her even though he told her he could never marry her because he must help his wife rear their children. She only knew she loved and was loved. Adam's arms around her was the only reality she wanted.

Rena now pulled her thoughts back to the problems of the present as she looked at her ringless hand resting on her desk. I can't think of either Taylor or Adam, she told herself. I've got to think about Mother. She says she wants to go home.

Rena glanced again at her bare fingers. Suddenly the answer to her problems was clear in her mind. "Mother, don't worry," she whispered. "I'm going to take you back to the ranch. The hell with everything else."

2

ADELHEID SCHWOPE, Rena's mother, grew up on a Rio Grande farm which bordered the Steiner farm. Both families had migrated from the midwest in the early 1900s and bought river bottom land. They pastured a few cattle and sheep for meat and grew abundant gardens in the summer that provided vegetables for the rest of the year. They cultivated grape arbors and soon found that the lush fruit could be made into a clear tasty wine that they could market. The money was sorely needed to supplement their meager incomes. Wine-making quickly became an important part of their farming operations.

The fair, blue-eyed Schwope girls worked by their parents' sides on the farm. There was never a time when they were carefree children. Chores lasted from early morning before the sun came up until the last cows were milked at dusk. They worked steadily without complaint and never cast a glance beyond the endless rows of crop land that had to be hoed and the plump bunches of grapes that had to be picked.

School was not an option for the Schwope children. They were too far from Socorro to attend classes there, and they didn't have the money, as some of the rural families did, to rent a house in town during the winter months so the children could go to school. But Kurt Schwope taught his children to read and do sums on Sundays after services. That was the extent of their education.

The family never attended formal church services, either. The only place of worship in Socorro was a Catholic Church, and the Schwopes were dedicated Lutherans, so they held Sunday services in their own home, and the neighboring German Lutheran Steiner family joined them. The two families read their Bibles together and consistently reaffirmed their church's beliefs.

Adelheid was one of seven Schwope girls. They all looked similar with their blonde braided hair and round blue eyes. They spoke only when addressed by their parents and conversed in muted voices with each other. Talking was considered a waste of time, so conversation was kept to a minimum.

But in spite of her self-effacing demeanor, sixteen year old Adelheid caught the eye of the young neighbor from the Steiner farm who attended the Sunday meetings. Rudy Steiner surprised Adelheid Schwope one morning after their worship service by asking her to accompany him to the grape arbor near their kitchen door to inspect the quality of the grapes.

"Heidi," Rudy said with a glint in his blue eyes. "I'd like to look at your concords. We aren't having much luck with ours this year."

Adelheid had never been called Heidi before. "You mean me?" she asked.

"Who else?" Rudy said, smiling.

A blush flooded the girls's face, and she looked frantically around for her father. Kurt Schwope caught his daughter's eye and motioned for her to go with the young neighbor.

She rose like a wooden puppet and followed Rudy Steiner as he headed for the kitchen door. The couple turned toward the thick grape plants that grew up and over the arbor that had been constructed with posts and wire. The rich purple fruit hung down in tantalizing bunches of perfection. Rudy reached for a grape and put it in his mouth. Adelheid did the same.

"Pretty good," Rudy said as he nodded his head. "But maybe it should be a little sweeter for good wine."

Addie chewed her grape thoughtfully and deliberately raised her head and looked straight into Rudy's eyes. "'Tis sweet enough," she said firmly. "Will make good wine."

"I like my wine sweeter," Rudy persisted.

Addie's eyes held steadfastly to Rudy's face as he moved closer to her. She felt a moment of panic as his strong arms enveloped her. His demanding lips found her tremulous mouth, and Adelheid felt herself slipping into a world she had never known.

Rudy finally released her and calmly finished chewing his grape. "It tastes better with the sweetness of your mouth," he said. Addie's lips remained slightly open, and warm grape juice threatened to roll down her chin from the side of her mouth.

Rudy wiped the corner of the girl's mouth with a broad thumb, licked the purple juice with his tongue, and threw back his head and roared with laughter.

Addie's senses were reeling from the first kiss she had ever experienced, and his wild merriment made her uncomfortable. She was confused because of these sudden developments and reacted with anger.

"What is so funny? Do you find me so ridiculous?" Addie turned to go, but Rudy's determined arms were instantly around her waist again, as she felt her slight body pulled tightly to him.

"No, no, my little summer squash. I find you the prettiest girl on the river, and I plan to marry you, Heidi Schwope." His lips again claimed their prize, and Addie felt as if she were being pulled up and over a rainbow. As she slid down the other side, she realized her fate was sealed. She knew she was destined to belong to Rudy Steiner.

Now as she sat slumped in Rena's car remembering her girlhood courtship of long ago, Addie sighed and turned her head toward the window as Rena passed a Highway 85 sign. "Are you all right, Mother?" Rena asked nervously.

"I'm fine," Addie said softly. "I'm going home."

"Just rest. We'll be there before you know it," Rena assured her.

Addie closed her eyes and her thoughts went back to the first years of being Mrs. Rudy Steiner. She had been prepared for married life as far as knowing how to work and pull her end of the load in keeping a farm going productively, but she didn't know how to please a husband's needs. She had a difficult time communicating with him, and often she didn't feel responsive to his love making. But she quickly learned it was best not to set off his quick temper, so she succumbed passively to the marriage bed and let her husband have his way.

Addie hadn't really gotten to know Rudy Steiner before she married him. At times she felt as if she were living with a complete stranger. She didn't understand his outgoing affectionate nature. She had been reared by undemonstrative people of few words who deliberately concealed their emotions. She didn't know how to respond to a person who openly showed and articulated his love for her. She felt she was losing her identity as her husband tried to entwine her being totally within his. There were times she felt stifled and wanted to push him away. She craved the ability to think her own thoughts and do her own things, and as time went by, she grew to resent his controlling nature.

The busy years passed, and Adelheid realized that Rudy had become discouraged with her and more involved with his work, and he left his silent wife to herself. He bought a ranch near Magdalena and spent much of his time there. Addie suspected he enjoyed the night life and bar maids of the wild saloons that flourished in the small western town. She didn't mind and was relieved when she was left to her own solitary life of peace and quiet.

The baby girl who had been born one year after their marriage changed their lives very little. She was a good baby who needed nothing beyond food and clean clothes. Adelheid could care for her without feeling her life intruded upon.

Addie suddenly opened her eyes and noticed the familiar landmarks of the river farms unfolding. "I'm nearly home," she said. "Thank God."

Rena sighed as she made the turn to drive the last mile to the ranch house. The sun was starting to sink behind the Magdalena Mountains to the west. It had been a long eventful day. She had visited her supervisor after talking to her mother and had requested a three month leave of absence. Her work record had been impeccable, and she had taken off little time during the twelve years she had worked there. The supervisor gave her the leave, although she worried about how she would fill the vacant work slot while she was gone. Rena had called Adam's secretary and left him a message, canceling their meeting that night. She had then rushed home and packed two small suitcases and a box of food before she had rushed back to the hospital and checked her mother out.

Rena had felt an empty, eerie feeling as she left the outskirts of the city and crossed the Rio Grande River. Suddenly she wondered if she were leaving her life here forever. The tears started to come, and she impatiently chastised herself. What's wrong with me? I'll be back. But the words came unbidden, "I wonder."

"What?" her mother had asked weakly from her side of the car.

"Just thinking about how much the city has grown since I moved here," Rena had replied quickly.

"Too much," her mother had muttered.

As they approached the ranch, Rena recognized the stucco Spanish style house located on the edge of alfalfa fields and fruit orchards. Past the horse pasture, the thick green bosque camouflaged the Rio Grande River that skirted their ranch as it wound its way southward. Rena caught her breath as memories of her beautiful childhood playground crowded out the anxiety of the day. A road runner ran along beside the car as they neared the house. After living in this setting for so long, it's easy to understand why Mother wouldn't have been happy at my home in Albuquerque, Rena thought.

Addie's eyes were now anxiously scanning the area to the south of the house where another home peeked through cottonwood trees. "I wonder if Boone's home. Honk your horn, Lorena," she instructed.

Rena gave three loud blasts of the horn. Of course her only thoughts are of Boone, she thought. They always were, and they always will be. But heaven only knows, I'm used to that.

A tall long-legged man came striding through the desert dust to greet the travelers. He waved and quickly opened the door for his mother. "I'm surprised to see you. If you had called, I would have come and gotten you."

Rena stepped out and walked around to greet her brother. "She's going to need help for a while, Boone. I've taken off some work time to stay with her."

Boone patted his sister's arm and nodded his head. "Well, that's doggone nice of you to do that. You know Darlene has her hands full with the kids and another one due soon."

"I know. Let's get Mother in the house. I'm sure she's tired."

"Sure thing," Boone said. "Come on, Mother. Let me help you."

The big man picked his frail mother up in his strong arms and carried her into the house. Rena walked ahead and went in the bedroom and turned down the blankets. Boone set his mother down gently on the bed and said, "Now you'll be comfortable, little Mother. After you've had time to rest a while, I'll come back and visit with you. Okay?"

Addie laid her head down on her pillow and said weakly, "Do come later, Boone. I need to talk to you."

Boone tiptoed out of the bedroom, and Rena pulled the covers over her sick mother. She looked exhausted, but there was a smile of satisfaction on her face.

"Rest for a while, Mother," Rena said as she kissed her lightly on the forehead. "I'll fix us some supper."

"I want Boone to come back," Addie said as she closed her eyes. "See that he's here."

"I will, Mother," Rena said with resignation as she turned to unpack the car and get settled into the old home.

They say you can't come home again, she thought to herself. Well, so much for those words of wisdom. Here I am!

3

RENA PULLED THE THROW RUG ASIDE and opened the trapdoor to the cellar under the kitchen. It had always been used to store extra food supplies. She climbed down the steps and felt the same uneasiness in the pit of her stomach she had always experienced as a child when she had gone down into this dark pit. She searched for the chain that hung from the bare light bulb. She then scanned the dirt walls for snakes, centipedes or water dogs. They had never been there, but she had always dreaded they would be.

As she looked around, she spotted the same cans of soup, tuna, and chili that had always been on the shelves. "I wonder how old they are," she muttered to herself. She soon found a partial basket of potatoes and onions and gathered up a few. "Aha! A jar of sour kraut! This will please her German soul." From the home-canned shelves she retrieved a pint of apricot preserves, and from a higher shelf she selected a cool smooth bottle of wine. "You're going to dine like a queen tonight, Mother," she said with satisfaction.

Before long Addie was looking down on the tempting meal Rena had prepared. She grunted her approval when she tasted the potato soup. She alternated bites of kraut and toast spread with apricot preserves. Rena smiled and thought, they just didn't know how to feed her in the hospital. The nurses had complained she wouldn't eat.

"You ate a good supper, Mother," Rena said as she picked up her tray. "I'll leave you to finish your wine and I'll be back in a little while to help you get ready for bed." She glanced back at her patient as she went out the door.

Adelheid was relaxed against her pillows, sipping her drink. The expression on her face was almost angelic. She thinks she's in heaven because she's back at home eating her favorite food and drinking her own wine, Rena thought. Bless her heart.

Rena ate the same supper that she had prepared for her mother, except she didn't finish up with a glass of wine. She had never liked the drink her parents made. Instead, she drank a cold glass of the milk she had brought from Albuquerque. She enjoyed every bite of her first supper back at the old home.

After cleaning up the supper dishes, Rena went back to her mother's bedroom. She helped her to the bathroom and steadied her while she washed her face and hands and brushed her teeth. Then she pulled a nightgown over her head and tucked her into bed. Addie lay back on the pillows as if exhausted.

"Sit up, Mother, while I brush and braid your hair," Rena said. "Then I'll get your pills for you, and you'll be all ready for a good night's sleep in your own bed. How about that?" Addie said nothing but sent a grateful glance her daughter's way.

As Rena settled her mother under her covers and gave her a kiss on the forehead, she said softly, "Sleep well, Mother." She was just leaving the bedroom when she heard the back door open and shut noisily. Then she saw the long length of Boone profiled in the kitchen light.

"Hi Sis!" came Boone's loud voice. Rena's first instinct was to tell him to be quiet, but she smiled instead as she went to meet her brother. Mother will be glad to see him, she thought to herself. He could always make her face light up.

"I just put her down for the night," Rena said. "She ate a good supper, and she seems to feel fine."

"Great!" Boone replied as he headed for the bedroom. "How ya doin', Mother?"

Rena walked into the living room and stretched out on the leather couch. It had been a long day.

There's Daddy's big chair, she thought as she glanced over to the matching leather recliner. She could almost see him sitting there with his pipe and his long legs stretched out in front of him. He would be talking and waving his pipe and wiggling his toes in his stocking feet. She could imagine his big laugh booming through the room. "Oh, Daddy, I miss you so much," Rena whispered as she felt the tears roll down her cheeks. "I don't know how I'm going to get through all this."

Pictures of her father swept into her mind. She remembered the tall cowboy in his riding clothes: tight levis, scuffed cowboy boots, plaid western shirt, red handkerchief tied around his neck, shiny silver buckle on his belt, big black hat pulled down over his eyes, white hair held back in a pony tail under the hat brim. Such a handsome man, Rena thought with a smile.

She remembered him mounting his horse. He would lift one long leg into the stirrup and throw the other over the saddle in one fluid motion. Grasping the reins with his left hand, he would sit for a minute straight and tall in the saddle as he backed his horse a few steps before moving off. Sometimes he turned him around in a circle a time or two. Then he would lean forward and give the mount his head as he urged him forward. With a smile and a wave he would be gone. He always rode a good fast horse. "He's not happy unless he's got one that will buck him off once in a while," her mother used to grumble.

And, it was on a bad horse that Rudy Steiner had met his death. He had bought the horse at the sale ring in Los Lunas and couldn't wait to try him out. He was a beautiful high stepping sorrel thoroughbred, and he and his rider made a perfect western picture as Rudy headed out on him early one morning to take a pack trip to the top of Ladrones Peak. "I'll have the vinegar out of him by the time he makes this climb," Rudy had told Addie.

But that proved to be Rudy's last ride, and the horse won that contest. About two thirds of the way to the top of the mountain where the trail was the steepest, the horse had thrown his rider off down the side of the mountain. A search group found Rudy five days later. His neck was broken. No one ever knew what happened to the thoroughbred.

Rena thought back on the call she had gotten in Albuquerque, telling her what had happened. The first thought she had after the initial shock was, that's the way he would have wanted to go. She still knew this was true, but it was so sad, as he was almost too alive to ever really die. "You must still be around here in some form, Daddy," Rena murmured.

Rena's thoughts moved on, and she reminisced about the later years of her father's life. What happened to you? she wondered. She remembered how he had started staying away from home more and more. Of course, he had the ranch at Magdalena to check on, but did he have to be gone so much?

And when he did come home, he was usually drinking. His red face and argumentative attitude would signal he had stopped at a bar either in Magdalena or Socorro. Alcohol always turned his affable personality into one of distrust and sarcasm. Rena remembered how she always managed to quickly vanish into her room when her father was in this condition. She would play her records loudly to drown out the heated discussions between her parents that lasted long into the night.

What happened? she wondered again. What changed my charismatic father into an embittered old man who drank too much?

Just then, Rena's eyes settled on the guitar and violin cases in the corner of the room. She slowly got up and walked over to the musical instruments. She hadn't looked at them since her father died. She and her father had played for many dances with that fiddle and guitar, and she hadn't been able to open the cases since.

Now she placed the violin case on the floor and unfastened the snaps. She opened the lid and gazed at the shining wood of the beautiful instrument lying inside. Gently she ran her fingers over the strings. She lifted the horse hair bow and pulled out one dangling hair. "Oh, Daddy," she said in a broken voice as she held the hair to her cheek. "The music you made on this fiddle brought happiness to so many people. If you could play Mother a piece now, she'd get well." She put the bow back in the case and gently closed the clasps. "No one else must ever play his fiddle," she whispered softly. "Anyway, no one could play it like he did."

Rena brushed her eyes and reached for the guitar case. This was the instrument she had played with her father to accompany his violin. She took it out and sat down in a chair, cradling it in her lap. She had buried her guitar playing with her father. She had felt no desire to make music after he died.

But now, Rena tentatively placed her fingers around the neck of the guitar, and they automatically fell into place for a chord. She strummed gently with her other hand. Other chords followed naturally, and the strumming continued. Rena smiled. It felt good to hold her guitar in her hands again. I've missed the music, she thought.

Rena was so engrossed with her strumming that she didn't notice Boone standing in the doorway. She was startled when he said, "It's good to hear you play again."

Rena laughed apologetically. "Sorry I jumped. I didn't know you were there."

"You were lost in it," Boone replied.

"Is Mother asleep?"

"Yep. My boring talk put her out."

"No, no. Whatever you say, she loves to hear it."

"I don't think that's true. Anyway, I wanted to say how good it is to have you here."

Rena looked up at her younger brother. They had never been very close, but she recognized the sincerity in his words. Standing up and putting the guitar carefully back in its case, she said quietly, "It's good to be here, Boone. You don't know how good it is."

Something in her face caused Boone to ask hesitantly, "Is everything all right, Rena? Do you need to talk? I could lend you one of these big ears."

Rena smiled at her brother who, she realized, was trying to be understanding with her. "Maybe I'll let you do that some time," she replied. "No, I'm just tired. It's been a long day. We'll talk about things later. I'm getting my bones to bed. Tell Darlene and the children I'll visit with them tomorrow."

"Sure thing," Boone said as he headed down the hall and out the back door. There was relief in his voice. He didn't really want to face any serious talks with Rena right now. He preferred to operate on a shallow, uncomplicated level with most people. He had enough serious concerns with his pregnant wife and his two demanding little girls. He needed no more problems, and he was very relieved that Rena was here to help with his mother. He whistled a few tuneless notes as he headed back to his house.

Rena sat down on the leather couch. He's a good boy, she thought.

Well, he's not a boy anymore; he's acting more mature now. He's finally really growing up.

Thoughts of Rudy Steiner pushed themselves back into her head. Suddenly it hit her. "Daddy changed after Boone was born," she said aloud. "That's when he started drinking and staying away from home so much. Why should that have been? He finally had the son he always wanted."

Rena mulled her thoughts over another minute, and then she sighed and headed down the hall. "Well," she concluded, "he probably didn't like the attention the baby got. Mother never knew anyone else existed after Boone was born. She neglected me, too, Daddy. But I didn't start drinking."

Rena glanced at her mother as she passed her room. Since she seemed to be resting quietly, Rena went on to her old bedroom, noticing the same frilly curtains and pink chenille bedspread. Her heartthrobs' pictures were still tacked up on the wall. Good old John Wayne and wonderful Elvis. You're still my favorites, she thought.

After she put on her flannel pajamas, the old bed looked so tempting. But she slowly dragged her feet down the hall to the bathroom to brush her teeth and splash her face with warm water. She looked at her reflection in the mirror and laughingly noted to herself that she looked like a blonde Rita Hayworth. "I wish," she said aloud with a toss of her hair.

The girl in the mirror looked back at her with sober eyes and seemed to say, "No, you didn't start drinking after Boone was born, Rena, but you left home as soon as you could, and you stayed away. You really weren't much different than your daddy."

4

THE BRIGHT AUTUMN SUN SHONE through the lace curtains of Rena's bedroom window and etched soft designs on her tousled hair spread across the pillow. She eased up from the deep cradle of the goose down in which she was buried and turned over and stretched. What a good sleep, she thought before she opened her eyes, and then she slowly looked around at the familiar pieces of furniture in her girlhood room. She noted the beauty of the lines and wood in the antique dresser and chest of drawers. This bedroom set had belonged to her Grandmother and Grandfather Schwope.

"Birdseye maple," she said aloud. "I never knew these antiques must be worth a fortune." She thought of the expensive modern set she had in her bedroom in Albuquerque. We paid a fortune for it, but it certainly doesn't have the quality of this one. She shook her head in amazement at this newfound realization.

I must have gone to sleep the minute my head hit the pillow, she thought with satisfaction. I haven't slept so well in years.

Rena then thrust her legs over the side of the bed. I'll check on Mother, she thought, and get a fire going for coffee and breakfast. She pulled on a pair of loose jeans and put on a comfortable shirt.

Walking barefoot down the hall, she looked in on her mother. Addie was so still Rena thought she was asleep, but then she noticed her eyes were open. "Morning, Mother. Did you sleep well?"

Addie slowly turned her head toward the door and said distinctly, "Yes, for the first time in months."

She wasn't in the hospital for months, but I suppose it seemed like months to her, Rena thought. "I'll make a fire and get the coffee on in a few minutes," she said.

She went on to the bathroom and splashed her face with cold water, ran a comb swiftly through her long hair and secured it with bobby pins in a roll at the nape of her neck. Hair like silver moonbeams, she thought as she smiled. That's what Adam says, but it's just a plain old bun today.

Rena then took her worn sturdy oxfords out of the closet and laced them up quickly. She glanced at her reflection in the mirror as she passed by the dresser on her way out of the bedroom. "Lorena Brooks, ranch woman," she said, opening her eyes wide in genuine surprise at the change in her appearance. "Anyway, no uncomfortable high heels for me today."

There was enough kindling in the wood box to start the fire in the range, and as it crackled to life, she put water and coffee in the same old blue pot her mother had used when she was a child. Another antique, she thought.

"While the coffee perks I'll bring more wood in," she told herself. She opened the back door and stepped out on the porch. Seeing a mocking bird perched on a low branch of one of the cottonwood trees, she remarked to him, "What a beautiful day." The bird stuck its tail up straighter, but made no response.

Rena headed over to the wood that was stacked under the trees. I guess I'd better do a little chopping, she thought. The cedar and juniper logs were cut in twelve inch lengths, but they needed splitting into smaller pieces.

As Rena picked up the ax, she wondered if she still remembered how to wield the tool. I used to be a good wood chopper, she thought. She remembered that she had prided herself on being able to hit the middle of the block and sometimes split the chunk of wood in two pieces with one stroke. "Good eye," her father had told her. "And strong arms." She had been proud of that compliment. What a tom boy I must have been, she now realized.

Rena selected a dry piece of juniper and set it on the chopping block. She raised the heavy ax and brought it down with accuracy on her target. She missed the center only slightly, and in three more strokes she had the juniper split into two pieces. She laid each piece in turn on the block and kept chopping until she had reduced the big piece of wood into several smaller sticks. She went through the same process until she had an armful of small kindling. This will make good fires, she thought as she carried the wood into the house.

The pungent smell of coffee greeted her when she put the wood in a basket by the stove. She picked up the teakettle and took it to the sink to fill it, pumping the handle several times before it brought up a gush of sparkly water. She had forgotten the relief one feels when the water actually comes out of the spout. She remembered a time growing up when the pump hadn't worked, and it was a stressful few days around the house until it was repaired.

Rena put the teakettle on one of the hot lids of the stove and raised the other lid and pushed more wood into the firebox. Then she went to check on her mother.

Addie was just climbing back into bed as Rena got to the door. "You should have waited for me to come and help you," Rena said. "You might have fallen."

"A person could wait for you forever, girl. And I didn't fall. Do you think I'm a baby?" The old woman looked at Rena petulantly.

"No, Mother," Rena said absently as she tucked in the covers around her mother. She must feel stronger, she thought. She took herself to the bathroom. And her color is better. But her bad disposition is definitely not improved.

"And don't bring my breakfast in here," the old woman said testily. "I'll get up and eat at the table."

"Of course, Mother." This is good news, she thought.

Soon the steaming teakettle told Rena she had hot water. She poured some in a small sauce pan to cook the oatmeal her mother ate every morning. She put bread in the wire toaster, laying it on the back part of the range. After one side browned, she turned it over so the other side would brown. Kind of a neat way to make toast, she thought as she smiled at the thought of what Adam would think if he saw her at this moment. He always took her to the most sophisticated places to eat. He probably had never visualized his expensively dressed lover as someone who could chop wood, make a fire, and cook breakfast on a wood range. I should tell him to rent a cabin in the mountains sometime and surprise him with my pioneer skills, she thought with a sparkle in her eyes.

Rena put butter and jelly and milk and sugar on the table and poured the hot porridge into thick bowls. She buttered the toast, cut it in halves, and put it on a saucer. She poured two glasses of orange juice and then filled two mugs with the rich brown liquid that had perked to perfection in the coffee pot.

When Rena went to get her mother, she found her sitting on the side of her bed. She had pushed her feet into house slippers. "Get me that robe hanging on the closet door," she ordered.

Rena quickly helped her mother put the robe over her nightgown. While assisting her to her feet, she was reminded again how slight and frail she felt. Addie had never been a big woman and could ill-afford to lose the weight that had gone as a result of her disease.

Rena kept her arm around her mother's waist and steadied her as they walked to the kitchen. She helped her sit down in her chair and then went to the other end of the table. She watched as her mother put two heaping spoons of sugar on the porridge and then reached for the cream pitcher with a trembling hand. Rena jumped to help her, but Addie waved her back and poured an uncertain stream of cream on the oatmeal. As she set the pitcher down unsteadily, she motioned toward the orange juice. "I don't want that. I want prune juice."

Rena sat down and said, "Mother, we don't have any prune juice. I'll get you some in town today." Her mother said nothing and concentrated on spooning bites of the warm cereal into her mouth.

"The oatmeal tastes good," Rena remarked. She hadn't eaten this kind of a breakfast in many years. "This will make me strong for the wood chopping I have to do today." Addie gave her daughter a straight look as she sipped on her coffee, but said nothing.

Rena had just finished her cereal and juice when a knock at the door interrupted their breakfast silence. She was expecting to see Boone, but to her surprise, a strange woman stood at the door. In answer to Rena's questioning look, the woman said, "Good morning. I assume you are Mrs. Steiner's daughter. I live on the Schwope place. Boone told me you were here, and I thought I would stop by and get acquainted and also see how Addie is doing. I'm Debbie Jaramillo."

Rena took the woman's hand. "I'm Lorena Brooks. Just call me Rena."

The short dark-haired young woman with a friendly smile came into the room. "How are you feeling, Mrs. Steiner?" she asked in a warm voice.

"Just fine," Addie answered shortly, continuing to eat her breakfast.

"Sit down and have coffee with us," Rena said, smiling.

Debbie sat down and rubbed her hands together. "Just what I need." She took the proffered steaming mug and repeated, "Just what I need."

As Debbie tried to talk to Addie, Rena listened with amusement to the one-sided conversation. I'm not the only one she doesn't talk to, she told herself. But Debbie seems to know her pretty well. She doesn't let her silence stop her.

Rena knew her mother had rented the Schwope house since her father had died. Before that, they usually had a hired man there. She was favorably impressed with her mother's neighbor who seemed to be pert, pretty, and self confident.

Debbie then turned to Rena. "I want to offer my help, Rena. I'm a nurse. I work in Dr. Campbell's office in town. If I can be of any help to you, let me know."

"Thanks, but . . . " Rena started to say she thought they would make it fine.

"I'm sure you will do fine," Debbie interrupted. "But if you ever need advice or just someone to talk to, I'll be available. You might even need someone to help you with shots or an enema or something like that."

"Oh," Rena said in a low voice, "An enema! I never thought of that!"

"Anyway, I'm so glad you're home, Mrs. Steiner," Debbie said with a warm smile directed at Addie's expressionless face. "Rena, I'll give you my doctor's office number and my home number, just in case. Don't hesitate to call if you need anything." Debbie handed Rena a card as she headed for the door. "I've got to be on my way. I hope you both have a good day." And with a cheery wave, Debbie was gone.

"Get me some peaches," Addie said as the door closed. "I've got to have some fruit in my stomach if my bowels are going to move. There should be a jar in the refrigerator."

Rena found the fruit and dished out a small amount for her mother. That's the most she's said to me, she thought as she placed the bowl in front of her mother. "I'll make your bed while you eat your peaches," she said as she turned and headed swiftly to the bedroom.

After tidying up her mother's room, Rena dug in dresser drawers until she found some loose pants and a warm sweater for her patient to wear. She reasoned her mother would feel better if she got out of her night clothes and put on some daytime attire.

"Would you like to sit in the comfortable chair in the kitchen by the window, Mother?" Rena asked after she had her dressed. "I'm going to be working outside for a while, and you can watch from the window."

A flicker of interest crossed Addie's face. "I would like that," she said in a stronger voice.

After Addie was settled in her chair with a warm blanket over her legs, Rena cleared the table and put the dishes in the sink. "If you need anything, you can wave to me," she said as she tied a bandana around her head and went gratefully out into the fresh air, drawing in a deep breath. "I doubt I'm cut out to be a nurse," she told herself. "I think this is going to take more patience than I have."

But when she attacked the wood pile, all negative thoughts left her. She loved the feel of swinging the ax through the air and watching it hit the target. She loved the sound of the wood splintering and the smell of the pitch permeating the air as the blocks split apart. I'm good at this, she told herself with satisfaction.

Once in a while the woodchopper glanced at the window. Her mother sat there unmoving.

After a while Rena leaned back against the cottonwood tree and wiped the perspiration from her forehead. "That's the first time I've worked up a sweat in a long time," she murmured with a smile.

Suddenly two giggling little girls appeared at the woodpile. Boone's little daughters had come to visit. She knew one girl was Merla and one was Marla, but she didn't know which was which. "Are you Merla?" she said to one of the girls who had a finger in her mouth.

"No," the tot answered breathily. "Her is Merla." She pointed her wet finger to her sister who was trying to turn a somersault in the chips.

A warm feeling suddenly engulfed Rena's heart. They're so cute, she thought. She had seen the children only once before, and she had paid no attention to them then. She and Taylor had stopped by the ranch for a few minutes after he had been a guest speaker at the college. "Then you're Marla?" she asked the child.

"Yeth," the little girl replied shyly. She took her finger out of her mouth and looked at it soberly.

Rena then leaned her ax against a tree and impulsively gave Marla a quick hug. "Do you know you are beautiful?" she asked as she knelt down.

"Dere's a 'tink bug," Marla said, changing the subject and pointing a wet chubby finger.

"Where?" Merla asked as she sat up after the successful completion of her somersault.

"Dere," Marla said as she pointed again.

Merla picked up a chip and pushed the bug off the piece of wood. He righted himself and immediately turned up his back end and stood poised for battle.

"Him goin' to 'tink!" Marla said in alarm. She moved back and looked fearfully at the bug.

"I will step on him," Merla said bravely, stamping down hard, but missing her target.

"Come on, girls," Rena said, taking them by the hands. "Come and say hello to your grandmother."

Merla looked back longingly at the beetle but followed her aunt's directions. When they got to the window, she was as excited to see her grandmother as she had been over the bug. "Granny, Granny," she yelled in a loud voice.

"Gwanny, Gwanny," Marla echoed in her shrill little voice.

Addie's hand slowly came up, and she moved her fingers slightly in a wave to her granddaughters. A small smile crossed her face.

"Gwanny is sick," Marla said in a sad voice. "Poor Gwanny."

"I feel sorry for her," Merla said in the same sad voice.

Rena looked from her mother's face to the two little girls waving frantically at the window. She knelt between them, putting an arm around their small waists. "You know, girls, your granny is sick. But I'm sure she feels better now that she has seen you two. Will you come to see her every morning about this time? I think you are the best medicine she can have."

Merla's face clouded up. "We not med'cine," she said.

"I hate bad med'cine," Marla said, puckering her face in distaste.

Rena laughed as she looked at the serious faces of her nieces. "No, darlings, you are not bad medicine, but you are the best medicine your granny has had in a long time. Now go home and tell your mommy that your auntie says you are good medicine for Granny." She kissed each puzzled little face and turned them in the direction of their house. "Come back to see us tomorrow morning. I'll help you make a playhouse in the woodpile."

"A playhouse?" Merla said wonderingly.

"A pwayhouth?" Marla repeated.

"Yes, I'll show you how to make tables and chairs and beds. Into her mind came a picture of the playhouse she used to build in this very woodpile. She would pull several blocks of wood together and put a towel over them for a table, and then she'd have tea parties with her dolls. There was a momentary pang in her heart for those days of fun and no responsibility.

The little girls ran giggling back toward their home. Rena watched them go with tender amusement. "What a pair," she said aloud. "Yes, you will be good medicine for your granny as well as for your auntie."

5

LATER RENA FED HER MOTHER A LIGHT LUNCH of chicken noodle soup, crackers, hot tea, and a chocolate cookie. The old lady was tired, so Rena helped her to the bedroom and tucked her in for an afternoon nap. Addie quickly closed her eyes and gave a sigh of relief as she nestled into her covers. She had spent more time up in the chair today than at any time during her hospital stay, and her frail body was spent and exhausted.

"I'm going to town to get you some prune juice, Mother. I'll have Darlene and the little girls look in on you while I'm gone. Is there anything else you want?"

"Pickles," was the soft reply.

"Pickles, Mother?"

Addie nodded her head, and Rena remembered the big jar of pickles her mother always kept in the refrigerator. She loved any kind of a pickle, but especially the sour ones. She must be feeling better to be getting her pickle craving back, she thought.

"Sure thing, Mother," Rena said as she left. "I'll bring you back some pickles."

Rena then walked over to her brother's home and knocked on the door. Her pregnant sister-in-law opened the screen and held it for her. "Hello, Darlene. I can't come in. I'm on my way to town to the grocery store. I won't be gone long. Could you check on Mother while I'm away?"

"Of course," Darlene replied. "I'm so glad you're here, Rena." She thrust out her hand and patted Rena's arm self-consciously. The two women didn't really know each other very well.

Rena looked at Darlene's swollen ankles and realized she'd better not be gone too long. It would be difficult for her to even walk over to the house, and she certainly couldn't take care of any emergency.

"Where's Boone?" Rena asked. "Over at the Magdalena Ranch?"

Darlene nodded. "He'll be back tonight," she said brightly. "He knows he can't be away too long now." She smiled and rubbed her protruding stomach.

As Rena started toward her car, she turned back to ask, "Do you think it's a boy this time?"

Darlene smiled with assurance. "Yeah," she called. "Anyways, it kicks like a boy!"

Rena got in her Buick, and as she headed up the lane, she thought, Darlene and I never have much to say to each other. Not much in common, I guess. But she seems to be a good wife and mother, and that's all that matters. She's not much to look at anymore, either, but probably Boone doesn't notice.

Darlene had been a perky little brunette when Boone married her. She came from a family of scant means and had barely finished high school. She was happy to capture a man after graduation. She had no aspirations for college or a career. The height of her ambitions was being Mrs. Boone Steiner and producing his children.

"Well, she has two cute little girls," Rena said into thin air as she cruised down the road. "And she's brought brunettes into the blonde Steiner family," she added with a smile.

Socorro looks like the same sleepy little town it has always been, Rena noted as she drove down the main street. She stopped in front of the grocery store, noticing its new front and paint job. The old store has been spruced up a little, she thought.

But there were the same familiar smells and sounds as she walked in the wide front entrance. Bertha was still swiftly punching the buttons on the cash register. There was a mixture of fruit, onions, and popcorn in the air. I must get myself a sack of that good popcorn, Rena promised herself. She got a basket and walked over to the last aisle and down the row of bottles and cans of juice. Things are kept in the same place they always were, she noticed with satisfaction, picking up two containers of prune juice.

Rena walked past the office which was located in the far end of the store where Clara, the bookkeeper, labored over the accounts, as always. Some things never change, Rena thought as she waved to the furrowed-browed lady. She hurried on and headed for the meat case.

Max, the butcher, still held court behind the glass counter. He was a white-haired old gentleman with a blood spattered apron pulled tightly over his large belly. He made his own hams and bacons and wieners and sausage, and customers came from far and wide to buy these delicacies.

Rena looked at the meat assortment in the display case. She didn't need any beef because she knew Boone kept her mother's freezer supplied with steaks and roasts and hamburger. So she bought some breakfast bacon and sausage. Then she saw some fat German sausages piled in one corner of the case. She knew they would be a real treat for her mother, so she bought four. She'll love these with sour kraut, Rena thought.

"Tell your mother this will make her feel better," the genial butcher said when he pushed the meat over the counter. "Welcome home, Miss Rena."

"Thank you," Rena said as a warm feeling engulfed her at being recognized.

I need pickles, she reminded herself and started up the middle aisle. She found the pickle display and put a jar of sour pickles in the basket and then added a jar of dills for herself. I'll get some mayonnaise, she thought, and I'll be able to make good sandwiches for both of us.

The cereal was in the next row, and Rena selected a box of grape nuts flakes and some shredded wheat. Her mother might need a change from her usual oatmeal.

A man was restocking the cereal shelves, so Rena steered her basket behind him, trying not to bump him. But the basket didn't steer very well, and the man turned with a startled face when she collided into him. Rena was embarrassed as she murmured a low apology without looking up and started to push the basket on down the aisle.

"Hold on," the man said as he reached out a big hand to stop the basket. "Lady, I'll have to turn you in as a hit and run driver if you don't stop and talk to me."

Rena stopped and raised a red face to the shelf-stocker. "I'm sorry," she said earnestly. "This basket is a little hard to steer. I'm so sorry."

Rena looked into the laughing face of a tall man with merry blue eyes topped by unruly curly red hair. Recognition started to dawn. It must be Shawn Murphy, she thought. I can't believe this.

"That's all right, Lorena," the man said as he engulfed her in his long hard arms. He looked down into her anxious eyes, and his infectious laughter bounced down the cereal aisle. Rena had a brief vision of cereal boxes falling off the shelves and dancing through the store.

Rena's face turned crimson red, and she reprimanded the big man who held her tightly in helpless immobility. "Let me go, Shawn. Everyone is looking."

The tight arms immediately unlocked their hold. "I'm sorry, Rena. I'm such an idiot, but I sure wasn't expecting to see you here today, darlin'. You're like a ghost materializing from the past."

Rena stepped back behind her basket. "Well, I'm not a ghost. I'm back here with my mother, and I'm taking care of her. I just brought her home from the hospital, and we needed a few groceries. I didn't expect to be attacked by a grizzly bear." She raised her chin, and the irritation was evident.

Shawn continued to beam at Rena in spite of her impatience, and she noticed the same two dimples that had always creased his cheeks. "So I'm a grizzly bear, huh?" he asked, laughing.

Tearing her eyes away from his dimples, Rena said coolly, "So you're still stocking shelves as you did in high school? Excuse me while I get some fresh vegetables."

Shawn then thrust his big body quickly in front of the grocery cart. "You can go only under one condition, and that is if you meet me at the drug store and let me buy you a cold drink before you go home." Rena started to shake her head, but he added quickly, "Just for old time's sake, Rena. Please. I'm sorry if I came across like an ignorant oaf, but I really want to visit with you. Just a short visit. I know you have to get back to your mother, and I have work to do myself."

"Well, all right," Rena said after a moment's hesitation. "I guess it's the only way I'm going to get out of here."

"I'll meet you in ten minutes at our old booth in the drug store," Shawn said with a smile.

Rena finished her shopping as contradictory feelings rushed through her confused mind. I must admit I'm glad to see him, she thought as her heart turned a little flip. But I must be pretty desperate to be swooning over my old high school flame.

She hadn't thought of Shawn Murphy for years. She had left him behind in her heart and in her mind when she graduated from high school, knowing she did not want to get trapped in Socorro. She wanted to marry a man who had some future and who could take her out to see the world. Then she had come home for a weekend after she started school in Albuquerque and met the college boy, Taylor Brooks, who was working on an engineering degree. She knew immediately that she had found what she wanted for a husband, and she forgot Shawn as she deliberately worked to entrap Taylor. She had never looked back. That Shawn Murphy even still existed surprised her. And yes, she had to admit it excited her just a bit.

Oh well, it won't hurt to have a Coke with him and visit a few minutes, she thought as she headed out of the store with her groceries.

The drug store still looked the same, too, she noticed as she entered. The soda fountain was on the left with several customers perched on red stools, enjoying cola drinks or ice cream. The right side of the store contained a large assortment of over-the-counter medicines. Farther back were shelves of jewelry and gifts. The druggist worked in a little cubby hole office in the back of the store.

Shawn was already seated in a booth just past the fountain. Two strawberry sodas were already colorfully decorating the table. He must have hurried right over, Rena thought.

Rena walked to the booth and looked from the sodas to Shawn. "You remembered," she said as she felt engulfed by feelings of nostalgia.

"Of course," Shawn said softly as he rose and towered over her. He lowered his head and looked into her eyes. "How could I forget my girl's favorite drink?"

"You have a good memory," Rena said as she quickly slid into the booth. Putting the straw into her mouth, she drew in a deep drink and gave an involuntary sigh of satisfaction. "It tastes heavenly."

"Not as good as the ones you used to make," Shawn said with a wink and a grin.

Rena quickly glanced around the big room. Yes, she remembered working here after school for three years while in high school. "I worked hard here," she said. "And I couldn't wait to get away and go to school in Albuquerque."

"I know," Shawn said a little sadly. "I missed you, Rena."

Rena said nothing. She couldn't honestly say she had missed Shawn.

"Tell me about your life," Rena asked, hoping to change the subject. "I heard you married and had a child."

Shawn set his glass down and raised serious eyes to Rena as he said, "Yes, I married Tina Glenwood. She was that cute little majorette who was a freshman when we were seniors. We were very happy, Rena." Shawn raised his drink and took a deep drag on his straw. He swallowed with an audible gulp.

"What happened, Shawn?" she asked softly.

Shawn raised stricken eyes and answered, "I lost her, Rena. She developed a rare disease and died last year."

"I'm so sorry," Rena said quickly. "She was too young to die. You must be very lonely."

"Yes," Shawn said slowly. "I miss her very much. But we have a daughter, and Suzie keeps me from being too miserable."

"How old is Suzie?" Rena asked.

"She's fourteen, and a little ball of fire. She's beautiful like her mother, and she likes to ride horses like her daddy."

"How nice. I'd like to ride with her sometime." For the first time Rena favored her high school friend with a glowing smile.

"That would be perfect," Shawn said. "She's thinking about running for rodeo queen next summer. Maybe you could give her some tips about queen competition. There was never a better rodeo queen than you were."

Rena's thoughts skipped back to the parades, the beautiful suits, and the attention. So long ago, it seemed. After a short pause, she said, "I'd love to work with Suzie. It would give me a chance to get out of the house and enjoy some riding again. It's been a long time since I've been on a horse."

Rena was aware of Shawn's intent look as he watched her face. He's wondering about me and my life, she thought. But he's not going to find out.

"I heard you were working at the University Hospital," Shawn said as he broke the silence.

"Yes," Rena replied. "I took a leave of absence to be here and take care of Mother. She wanted to come home to die."

Shawn reached across and put a big hand over Rena's. "I'm sorry, Rena. Life can be very hard at times. You're a good girl to come home with your mother."

Rena smiled and said nothing. She knew tears were close. For the second time in a few days she had been called a good girl. She felt a sharp stab of guilt as she suddenly acknowledged to herself that she had come home, not primarily to be with her mother, but rather to get away from her own personal problems.

Shawn sensed Rena's turmoil. Withdrawing his hand, he said quietly, "Well, I've got to get back to the store, and I know you have to get home. After you've had time to get settled down at the ranch, I'll give you a call and we can talk more about Suzie working with you."

As Rena and Shawn passed the soda fountain, a girl at the cash register took the money for the sodas and said, "Thank you, Mr. Mayor. Come back soon."

"See you again, Ruthie," Shawn called politely as he took Rena's arm. "I'll walk you to your car," he said with a warm smile.

Rena said nothing until they stopped by her car door. "So you're the Mayor of Socorro?"

Shawn looked down at the blonde woman by his side. "I guess so," he drawled. "I got elected last April. Don't really know why anyone would vote for me for mayor, but they did."

Shawn opened the car door for Rena, and she slid in. She looked up at him and said, "It was good to see you, Shawn, and thanks for the strawberry soda. Or perhaps I should say, thank you, Mr. Mayor, for the treat."

Shawn grinned and his ruddy complexion turned redder. "No," he said as he lowered his head in embarrassment, "that's not necessary. I'm still

Shawn to everyone. And, by the way, there's one more thing you should know. I'm not just a shelf stocker in the store."

"No?" Rena said lightly. "Don't tell me you own the store."

"You got it," Shawn smiled as he turned to go. "I'll call you one of these days." Rena knew he was smiling at the dumbfounded look on her face.

In her rear view mirror she watched the big man walk with quick steps back up the street. There was purpose and self-confidence in his step as he headed toward his store.

"Who would have thought it?" she asked herself. Shawn, the star basketball player who would have flunked high school if she hadn't helped him with his assignments, was now Socorro's leading citizen and businessman. "Time does change everything," she murmured to herself.

As Rena headed for home, she remembered the days she had strutted down this very street in her short white skirt and her cocky head majorette hat, the red tassels on her white boots bouncing to the beat of the high school band. "I was the prettiest girl in town," she said smugly. "But I couldn't wait to get away. What was I thinking? If I had stayed here and married Shawn, life would have been a lot more simple."

Concern for her mother suddenly pushed the image of Shawn Murphy from her mind. "I've got to hurry home," she anxiously reminded herself.

6

RENA PULLED UP IN THE YARD in a cloud of dust. So much for paved driveways, she thought. She honked the horn two times to let Darlene know she was back and then gathered up her groceries. Her mother was sitting at the window with an irritated expression on her face. "Obviously I'm not pleasing you, Mother," she said between her teeth, "but when did pleasing you ever happen anyway?"

As Rena struggled through the door with two heavy bags, the phone rang. She put the groceries on the kitchen table and leaped for the persistent little black device hanging on the wall. "Hello," she said breathlessly.

"Rena," came a relieved voice. "How are things going? I've been trying to get you all afternoon."

"I'm fine," Rena said. It's Adam, she realized, not feeling happy to hear his voice.

"I thought you might give me a call," the faraway voice continued.

"I haven't had time," Rena replied. "I'm trying to get things going smoothly here."

"You didn't even leave me your number," he said plaintively. "I had to check hospital records to get your mother's phone number."

"Well, I was in a tizzy," Rena said. "This all came on me pretty suddenly."

"I know, sweetie." Adam's voice was now soft and placating. "You're going to need help. Shall I hire someone to take over for you?"

"No. I'm going to take care of my mother myself," Rena said quietly.

"But how can you do everything by yourself?" Adam persisted.

"I have people to help me."

"A little child answered the phone when I called before. Is that one of your helpers?"

Rena didn't like the tone of his voice. "Well, perhaps she is, Adam. At any rate, I'm fine, and I don't want or need your help. Thanks for calling, but I haven't time to talk right now. I've got to fix some food for my mother."

Rena hung up and heaved a sigh. The world she had shared with Dr. Harrington seemed long ago and far away.

"I have a treat for our supper, Mother," Rena said loud enough for Addie to hear. "How would you like some German sausage and sauerkraut?"

"All right," Addie replied, and quickly added peevishly, "you were gone a long time."

"Well, I saw Shawn Murphy and we talked for a few minutes. He tells me he's the mayor of the town now, and he's also a grocery store owner. He's done pretty well for himself."

"Should o' known you'd find a man to talk to," Addie said sarcastically.

Rena ignored the remark and pumped water into a pan to cook the sausages. She felt the stress building and her patience diminishing.

Addie watched every move Rena made, and when she started to put the sausages in the water, she said in a louder voice than usual. "Don't put those sausages in water. Put them in the skillet."

Rena turned and looked straight at her mother as she tried to keep the irritation out of her voice. "Mother, I was going to boil them and then pour off the greasy water before I added the sauerkraut. That would be a more healthy way to eat them."

"They wouldn't have no taste that way," Addie protested. "Cook 'em the way I said."

"Yes Mother," Rena said as she took the iron frying pan from the warming oven. What does it really matter anyway? Rena thought. She might as well eat what she wants as long as she can.

Addie ate a good supper and seemed in a better humor as she watched her daughter clear off the table. "Did you enjoy your meal, Mother?" Rena asked.

"Um-huh," Addie grunted.

I wonder if she remembers how to say thank you, Rena mused. But, she never did use those two words much.

"That phone rang all afternoon," Addie said in a complaining voice. "We're going to have to take that thing out. I can't stand that noise all the time."

"I'm sorry, Mother," Rena said in a soothing voice. "I'll be here most of the time to answer it."

At that moment there was a knock on the door, and Debbie Jaramillo came in. "Thought I'd stop by and see if you need any help," she said cheerfully.

"Yes," Addie said before Rena could answer. "My bowels ain't moved in two days. I need a enema."

"We'll take care of that little problem," Debbie said quickly. "I'll go get my bag out of the car and be right back."

"It's good to have someone around here that knows how to do somethin'," Addie muttered.

"Let's get her to the bedroom," Debbie suggested when she came back in the house. "Then bring me a pan of warm water and some soft towels, and I'll take care of everything."

Thank God for Debbie, Rena thought.

Thirty minutes later Debbie returned to the kitchen where Rena was finishing the dishes. "Everything's all taken care of," she said, smiling. "She's ready for a good night's sleep. I gave her the pills, too."

"Thank you seems inadequate, but I do thank you so much, Debbie."

"All in a day's work," Debbie said as she patted Rena's arm. "One more thing. Don't let it get to you when she says hateful things. She's a very ill woman, and she has to take it out on someone. You're the chosen one!"

"So I've noticed."

"Actually, Rena, you have a very rare opportunity of being with your mother and taking care of her at this unique time in her life. You'll be happy you did after it's all over. Don't get discouraged."

Rena fought back the tears. "I think it's going to be very hard," she whispered.

"Life is hard, Rena. Hang in there." Debbie gave Rena a quick hug. "I've got to go, hon. Ernesto will be coming home for supper soon. There's nothing quite as scary as a hungry man wanting supper if it's not ready."

Rena felt guilty for keeping Debbie so long. "Oh, but wait a second." She opened the refrigerator door and took out the package of German sausages. "Take these home for supper. You can cook them fast. I got them for Mother, but she'll never eat all of these."

"Thank you!" Debbie said earnestly. "This will simplify supper."

Debbie was gone with a swirl of her white skirts, and Rena sat down in her mother's easy chair and closed her eyes. It had been a busy day. "I wonder if I can do this?" she whispered. "What have I gotten myself into?"

I haven't prayed very much in a long time, Rena realized. Suddenly she felt like getting down on her knees and pouring her heart out. She fell on the floor and buried her head in the cushion of her mother's chair. She let the muffled sobs flow freely for a while. Finally she said softly, "Dear Lord, I'm so sorry for everything. I'm so sorry I haven't been the daughter I should be. I'm so sorry I haven't been a good wife. I guess I did nothing right but maybe my work. I need your help, Lord. I don't know what I'm doing. I know I'm not a very good nurse. I know this is going to be so hard. But be with me, Lord. Be with my mother during this bad time. She needs you, too, Lord. I guess what I'm saying is that we can't do this by ourselves. Be with us, Lord, and help us, please."

Rena remained on the floor for several minutes as she continued her prayer. When she finally got up, her heart felt lighter. Now I don't feel so alone, she thought.

She tiptoed down the hall and checked on her mother and then went into the living room where she softly closed the door. She took her guitar carefully out of the case and quietly strummed it as peace seemed to flow back into her weary body and mind. Rena suddenly wanted to sing. "Thank you, God, thank you," she said, as she started humming verses of songs she remembered from Sunday School. Quickly the words to a chorus clarified in her mind.

"Wide, wide as the ocean,
High as the heavens above,
Deep, deep as the deepest sea,
Is my Savior's love.
I, though so unworthy,
Still I'm a child of His love,
For His Word teaches me that His love reaches me
Everywhere"

At that moment the phone interrupted her singing, and Rena rushed down the hall to pick up the receiver before the rings woke up her mother. "Hello," she said breathlessly.

"Rena?" a distant voice came over the line.

"Yes, this is Rena. I can hardly hear you. Who is this?"

"Taylor, of course. We must have a bad connection."

"Oh, hi Taylor," Rena said, surprised that she felt almost glad to hear his voice.

"I haven't been able to reach you at home, so I called the hospital, and they told me you had asked for a leave of absence to take your mother home. You could have told me your plans, you know." The bad connection didn't camouflage the irritation in Taylor's voice.

"I'm sorry. I should have called you. But everything's been so hectic." All I do is tell people I'm sorry, Rena thought.

"Well, let me know how your mother gets along. I'll be tied up here for a few more weeks. I'll let you go now. I know you are busy."

Rena hardly had time for a goodbye before the connection was broken. She hung up the phone and thought, so what's new about that? Taylor never really has time for me. I'm surprised he called.

Rena went back and picked up her guitar again and started thinking of some of the old songs she and her father had played. There was *Red Wing, Isle of Capri, Little Girl Dressed in Blue, Darling Nellie Gray, Maggie, My Grandfather's Clock*. The songs were coming fast to her mind. She started singing *Golden Slippers*, and it almost seemed as if her father were right there with her waiting to join in with his fiddle.

At that moment her brother appeared in the doorway. Rena stopped singing with a startled gasp.

"Sorry," Boone said in his deep voice. "You didn't hear me knock, so I just came in. Wanted to check with you and see how things are going."

Rena quickly laid her guitar down on the couch. "Mother had a good day, I think. You can't always tell by what she says as to how she feels. But she sat up part of the day, and she ate pretty well."

"That's great," Boone said enthusiastically. "I'm sure you're just what she needs."

"Well, I don't think I'm the best nurse in the world, but hopefully I can figure out this job. Debbie came over and helped. She's a nurse, you know."

"I know. She's a good lady and good at her job. Would you like for her to stop by regularly to help you? I think the ranch can afford to pay her. I'd just count it as ranch labor on the books."

Rena hadn't thought of that, but it made perfect sense.

"You know, Boone, I think that's a very good idea. You put me in an office and I feel very much at home, but being a nurse is a whole different scenario. I need all the help I can get."

"I realize that, Sis, and I also know that neither Darlene nor I can help you that much. I'll be taking cattle to market all this next month, so I'll be gone more than usual. And you know what Darlene will be doing. I was thinking of talking to Debbie about keeping an eye on her, too. It's pretty handy to have a nurse living close to us at this time."

"Do you want me to talk to Debbie about this?" Rena asked.

"You do that. You take care of it. That'll be a load off my mind." Boone got up and laid a big hand on the top of Rena's head. "It's good to have you here, Sis. I feel like I've got some good help now."

Boone pointed to the guitar. "Are you getting practiced up on that thing again?" he asked.

"Yes, a little bit. Look at my fingers." She turned her hand over and showed him her red calloused finger tips.

"Well, keep playing. I've missed your music. The little girls would love it, and Mom should enjoy it too."

"I doubt that," Rena said shaking her head. "She'd like it if you'd sing to her."

"No, she wouldn't," Boone corrected her with a zesty laugh. "I didn't get your talent." He turned to go. "Goodnight, Sis. Tell Mother I was here."

After Rena heard the back door shut, she sat in silence for a while. Prayers do get answered! she thought. I asked God to help me, and he's done it already. I can do this. I can do it with Debbie's help, and with your help, God. Thank you so much!

7

THE ARRANGEMENTS WERE MADE. Debbie would stop in at the Steiner Ranch every morning at seven o'clock before she went to work and every evening at seven o'clock after she came home. She could use the extra $200 a month, as she and her husband were trying to save up enough money to buy their own small ranch.

Rena felt less stress now that she could rely on Debbie to make the medical decisions. She concentrated on cooking tempting meals for her patient and thoroughly cleaning the old house that had collected dust and junk for years. Her mother never had been the best housekeeper even when her health was good. Drawers needed cleaned out, and closets of old clothes needed to be boxed up. Shawn helped her haul off the sacks and boxes of miscellaneous articles, some to the garbage dump and some to distribution centers for needy people.

In her cleaning chores, Rena unearthed some treasures she had forgotten she even had. She found her majorette boots, now turned up at the toes and yellowed with age and some of the clothes she had worn in high school. They were limp and discolored and rumpled from being packed away in boxes for twenty years. I'm surprised Mother held on to these. I didn't think anything of mine would hold any emotional value to her, she thought. Rena shook her head in puzzlement.

One box contained her jewelry, belts, purses, and coins. "Here's my Indian Head Penny Collection!" she said out loud. "Some of these coins must be worth a little money now." She poured the contents of the box out on a chair so she could carefully go through everything.

Most of the jewelry was worthless and she tossed it in a garbage sack. She hated costume jewelry now and wore only expensive gold or silver. Rena picked up an envelope, and a heavy chain fell out. A tarnished basketball dangled from it and she held it closer for inspection. Shawn gave this to me, she remembered. I wore it around my neck for two years. It's a wonder it didn't turn my neck green!

Then a small black book with gilded pages caught her eye. "Oh, here's some reading material!" she said happily. "My diary!" That was the end of the cleaning for a while. Rena settled down in a comfortable chair and started reading.

Most of the entries were about boys, which was not surprising. Rena had been boy-crazy in high school. There were pages about Jerry Pat. He was the handsome ranch boy she had always admired. There were numerous comments about him. "He smiled at me today." "He walked with me from gym class." "He sat by me in study hall." When she finally finagled a date with him, she remembered he was half drunk when he picked her up in his flashy red convertible. They had gone to a show and then parked in the bosque down by the river until the early hours of the morning. Her parents had been furious when she got home, but all she had done was listen to Jerry Pat snore for hours. His drinking had made him a very boring date. Her interest had quickly faded. She remembered that he had married young, but the marriage hadn't worked out. Too much money, too little responsibility, she concluded in her mind. Too bad. He was my dream cowboy!

There were entries about an older fellow she had gone with for a while when she was a senior. He was working on a construction crew that stayed in town for a couple of months. Her parents didn't know anything about Ray Mason. They would never have let her date him because of his age. But she saw him often under the pretense of visiting girl friends or attending ball games. Sometimes she was with him when she was supposed to be working at the drug store. They had even gone to Albuquerque one Saturday. What an adventure that was for the small-town Socorro girl!

The pages containing details of her romance with Ray were written in shorthand. She knew her mother read her diary, so she had to be careful about what she put in it. "Made mad love," she had written after the

Albuquerque trip. She smiled as she read it. She remembered they went to the zoo and sat for a while in Rio Grande Park. They had to hurry back so she could be home at the usual time after work. He was a nice guy, she thought. He never took advantage of me.

She remembered the letter she had received from Las Cruces after Ray's crew had moved on south. "I love you, Lorena," he had written. "I would like to marry you when you graduate. I have a good job, and I could take care of you."

The proposal had scared her nearly to death. She had torn the letter into a thousand pieces and buried it in the soft dirt near the woodpile. Her father would have killed her if he had known someone wanted to marry her! "I was pretty young when I got my first proposal," she murmured. She never answered that letter, and she never heard from Ray again.

As she put the diary in the box of things she was saving, she realized the reason her mother had never trusted her with the opposite sex. The entries in there were enough to incriminate me, and if Mother could have read shorthand, I would have been sent to a convent! she concluded.

"Oh well," Rena said as she stood up and tossed back her gleaming hair. "I had fun, but I kept my head and didn't go too far." She remembered a girl in her class who had dropped out of school because she became pregnant. She had seen her once a few months later, all bloated and swollen. The picture of the distended stomach remained frozen in her mind's eye and caused her to be determined to keep her romantic adventures to a minimum. Thereafter she strongly rejected any sexual propositions. It wasn't because of her mother's admonitions. All she had to do was think of poor Carmen and her enormous belly.

Rena then dumped the sacks of worthless mementos of her long gone past on the garbage heap and headed back to the house. It was time to fix mother's lunch.

Addie was staying in bed most of the time now. Debbie made her sit in a chair for a few minutes in the morning when she changed her bed and bathed her. She was always tired out by the time she got back in her bed.

"Her strength is going fast," Debbie told Rena. She had brought her a walker, but the only time she used it was when she went to the bathroom. It seemed to be a matter of pride with her to use the toilet instead of the bedpan.

"I've been cleaning out the back room," Rena told her mother cheerily as she delivered lunch to her bedroom. "This afternoon I'll sweep and scrub everything, and then it'll be in good shape."

"What are you throwing away?" Addie asked, suspicion in her voice.

"Just some of my old high school stuff," Rena replied. "I didn't know you had kept it."

"Don't throw the magazines away," Addie said sharply.

"Why?" Rena asked. "They must be very old and of no use now."

"Don't argue with me. Don't throw them away."

"All right, Mother."

In her mind, Rena knew that the magazines certainly would end up in the trash bags that day.

Marla and Merla came trooping in the house at that moment. Their two smiling cherubic faces blew away the tenseness in the room.

"Gwanny, we tum to see you," Marla gushed as she stuck her face down in her grandmother's soup bowl. "What you eatin'?"

"Soup, what do you think?" Addie replied impatiently. Casting a beseeching look in her daughter's direction, Addie said, "Go feed these children, Rena. Their mother never feeds them enough."

"Come on, girls," Rena said with a laugh. "Let's see what we can find in the kitchen."

The girls tumbled after Rena and were soon sitting at the table dipping cookies in milk. Rena sat down with them and had a bowl of soup left over from the pot she had made for her mother.

"You got garbage in the wood pile," Merla stated.

"Yes, I'm cleaning house and that's just old stuff that needs to go to the dump."

"Now we can't make a play house," Merla complained.

"No, we tan't make a pway house," Marla repeated.

"Yes we can, darlings," Rena assured them. "When the garbage is gone and Auntie Rena has time."

Speaking of garbage, Rena thought as she looked out the window, there's Shawn now with his truck.

"Finish your food, girls. I'm going outside for a little while. I'll be back in a few minutes." She knew her mother could hear their conversation and didn't want her to know that Shawn had come to haul away the junk. She might put a hold order on the whole operation!

Rena slipped on her work gloves and quickly headed out the back door. She greeted Shawn with a smile, and they began loading the sacks and boxes. "This is so nice of you," she said. "But we've got to hurry before Mother knows what I'm doing."

"She wants to save all her treasures?" Shawn asked with a grin.

"Oh, she's a real packrat," Rena said with a sigh.

The truck was loaded and on its way within a few minutes, and Rena hurried back into the house. The girls were just finishing their cookies and were still sipping their milk.

Rena went to check on her mother who was lying back on her pillow with her eyes closed. She noted that not much food had been eaten. "Mother," she said softly. "Open your eyes and take a few more bites of your lunch."

Addie opened her eyes and looked vacantly past Rena. "Where you been?" she asked.

"Just outside for a minute. Now take a bite of this tapioca pudding."

Addie obediently opened her mouth. How does she know everything that goes on? Rena wondered impatiently.

Rena spooned three more bites into her mother's mouth, and then it closed with authority. "No more," she said firmly.

"The girls will be in to tell you goodbye," Rena said as she carried the tray back to the kitchen.

"Girls, Granny is going to sleep. Go tell her goodbye, and it's time for you to go home. Auntie Rena has some things to do."

The girls tiptoed to their grandmother's door and peered in cautiously. "Bye, bye," Marla said softly.

"Goodbye, Granny," Merla said. "We're goin' home now."

The girls waited breathlessly until their grandmother opened her eyes and lifted one hand in a slight wave. Then they turned and ran giggling through the kitchen. They're glad to get out of this house, Rena thought. They're beginning to sense the anxiety here.

Rena then went back to the room where she had been working all morning. Those piles of magazines are going to be cleared out, no matter what, Rena thought. They date back years and years. Why is she saving these relics?

Rena picked up a few magazines gingerly and shook them to get the dust off. She remembered that sometimes her mother would stick a letter or a recipe in a magazine while she was reading it. Perhaps she should check.

Rena shook magazines and then sneezed from the dust she was creating. This is ridiculous, she thought. There couldn't be anything of any value in these magazines. But suddenly a picture fell out on the floor. It was a five by seven photo in amazingly good condition. "It's me!" she said in surprise.

She picked up the picture and looked at a young girl standing with her horse by an apple tree. The sun glinted off the crown circling the western hat of the cowgirl. Her laughing face was turned toward the handsome white blazed head of a sorrel horse whose soft eyes mirrored adoration for his mistress. "That's when I was rodeo queen," Rena realized as she studied the picture. "That was my red, white, and blue suit. The hat was red, the suit and boots were blue, the shirt was white, the tie was red, and my crown had red, white, and blue gems in it. Oh, I thought I was fancy!"

Rena was surprised at her striking beauty at that time. Her soft blonde hair was gathered in a tight ball of curls on the side of her neck. Her large blue eyes reflected the anticipation of all the wonder and adventure of this new phase of life into which she was emerging. I couldn't wait to meet and beat the world, Rena remembered. My daddy always said I was a "good feeler." I didn't know then what I was heading for, or I would have been a lot more sedate.

It's a good picture, she thought as she brought her eyes back to the rodeo queen. I remember the day Daddy took that picture out under the apple tree. We were getting ready to load up my horse to ride in the parade at the fair in Albuquerque. But I never saw the picture after it was developed. Mother must have put it in this magazine and forgotten it. Well, this is one good find.

Rena laid the picture aside and continued going through the rest of the magazines. She was almost to the bottom of the pile when some papers fell out. She picked up what appeared to be three folded notes. They were yellowed and crackly as she carefully unfolded them.

There wasn't much writing on the papers. The words were written in pencil and very faded, but she could make out the message, "See you tomorrow at the same place. Love, B."

Rena slowly unfolded the next note and read the sprawled writing aloud. "I'm the luckiest man in the world. See you Saturday. Love, B."

Rena creased her forehead and wondered aloud, "Who wrote these notes? They must be my mother's. They're in her magazines." She hesitated to open the last note. For the first time she felt as if she were intruding into someone's private life. But there was no turning back now. She deliberately unfolded the remaining paper. This one was dated, "4-15-50." The words said, "He knows. I must go. Love you always. B."

Rena sat on the floor in shock amid the magazines she was sorting. Instinctively she knew there was a significant meaning to these notes. They must have come to her mother. She must have hidden them so she would always have them.

There must have been another man, Rena reasoned. But that thought seemed so contradictory to the cold unapproachable image she carried of her mother. She never loved anyone but Boone. There couldn't have been another man, she assured herself.

Suddenly Rena didn't want to think of this mystery any more. She hastily gathered up the remainder of the magazines and thrust them swiftly into bags. She didn't want to know what might be hidden inside them. Let the secrets be burned with the magazines, she thought with a shudder.

Rena carried the bags of magazines out to the woodpile and dumped them on the ground. Shawn had told her he'd be back tomorrow to pick up any other trash. He was also bringing his daughter for her first riding lesson.

That will be fun, she thought as she tried to rid her mind of its troubling suspicions. It will be nice to be doing something in which I have real expertise instead of struggling with all these unfamiliar chores.

The phone was ringing when she got back in the house. I can't answer it, she thought. I can't talk to Taylor or Adam, but it will wake up Mother if it keeps ringing. Gingerly she picked up the phone. "Hello," she said uncertainly.

"Hi, Rena. Shawn here. Suzie wants to come in the morning for her riding lesson. The band will be marching tomorrow afternoon before the football game, and she has to do her majorette thing. Would it be all right if we came out about nine thirty?"

"It will be wonderful!" Rena said with relief. "I'll look forward to seeing both of you."

Rena sat down at the kitchen table. She didn't go back into the room and the notes that had made her feel so uncomfortable and confused. I must make a list of the points I'll go over with Suzie tomorrow, she thought, deliberately delegating a demanding project to her mind.

Taking a pencil and a piece of paper out of a drawer, she started writing:

SADDLE FORM

1. Sit up straight, toes pointed ahead in the stirrups, heels down. Weight on the balls of your feet.

2. Hold reins in left hand, one rein on either side of the ring finger.

3. Your weight should be evenly distributed in the saddle. Lean back slightly when horse lopes.

We'll discuss these points, she planned silently. Later on I'll drill her on how to keep her horse in the proper lead and how to wave like a rodeo queen. Oh, this is going to be fun!

Rena laid the pencil down and tipped her head back contemplatively. "Heck with those damn notes," she blurted out when the suspicious doubts returned to intrude on her thoughts again. "I'm going to be a riding instructor!"

8

"SHE WAS VERY COOPERATIVE," Debbie said as she sipped her morning coffee with Rena. "I made her walk down the hall after I got her bed changed. She tries, but it's getting harder for her. I gave her a little therapy today, also. I made her do some hand and arm exercises. And I massaged her feet and legs. They're getting swollen from inactivity.

"You're doing wonders for her, Debbie," Rena said gratefully. "I think she looks forward to your visits."

"Everyone likes attention," Debbie said with a smile. "Your mother has always been a very independent woman, but the time has come, and she knows it, when she needs help. This is a fine thing you are doing to stay here with her."

"Sometimes I wonder if she even wants me here," Rena said, sighing.

"Of course she does," Debbie assured her. "She knows what the alternative is, and she wants to stay home. All elderly people want to do that. The government is starting to get some programs going which will provide help for this type of situation. Older people with terminal illnesses will live longer and happier at home rather than in a public institution, whether it's a hospital or rest home."

Rena shook her head as she put her coffee cup down. "Well, I try, but I worry about being a good nurse. I've just never been in this situation before. Sometimes I really don't know how to handle things."

"You're doing very well," Debbie said as she got up from the table. "Hang in there. Whatever she says, let it run off like water from a duck's back. She really means, 'I'm so glad you're here taking care of me.'"

"Well, I am glad to be here with her. But . . . "

"No buts," Debbie interrupted. "By the way, you'll be seeing traffic coming and going at my house today. We're having a matanza. It's time to kill the hog and have a celebration. Ernesto has been up since dawn getting things started."

"A matanza!" Rena said in a delighted voice. "I haven't even heard of that event in years." She knew this was a day of feast and celebration, dating back to the early Spaniards who settled the country. "So Ernesto keeps the traditions going, huh?"

"Oh yes," Debbie said with a laugh. "It's fine with me. I don't do much of the cooking. He and his mother take care of that. They've got the hog roasting by now and have fed the brothers and their families breakfast. The coffee pots are steaming, and the hot chocolate pan is bubbling. Scrambled eggs and tortillas are being enjoyed by all. And the pinto beans and chicarrones are already on the fire."

Rena could visualize the scene. Ernesto's Spanish relatives and friends would be there, laughing and talking and dipping their pig skin chicarrones in red or green chili as they ate the delicacies, all the time gesturing expressively with their hands. It was a social ritual that not only served the purpose of feeding people, but it also preserved and maintained lifelong bonds of extended family and friends. Debbie was not Spanish, but she enjoyed the celebration and understood its meaning to her husband and relatives.

"Why don't you come over and join in the festivities?" Debbie asked. "Boone said he might stop over this evening when he gets back from the other ranch. Of course, he can't leave Darlene alone too long."

"I've got Suzie Murphy coming out for a riding lesson today," Rena said. "So I'm tied up all morning. Then there's lunch for mother, and I read to her until she goes to sleep in the afternoon. Also, I've got a little more cleaning to do on the back room. Then it'll be supper time for Mother, so the day is pretty full, really."

"Try to come over in the evening for a little while after we get your mother to bed," Debbie said. "I hear you do a good job playing the guitar and singing."

"Who told you that?" Rena asked.

Debbie laughed. "Actually, it was Shawn. I talked to him a while at the store yesterday, and I invited him out. He told me to try to get you over for some playing and singing."

"That rascal," Rena said, laughing. After a moment's hesitation she said, "Okay, I suppose I could run over for a little while when you're getting Mother ready for bed. It does sound like fun."

"See you later," Debbie said with a smile as she went out the door.

Rena reached for a sauce pan and filled it with water for her mother's cooked cereal. She noticed herself humming as she put the bread in the toaster. *"Oats and toast and grape jelly,"* she sang in a merry voice. *"Oats and toast and grape jelly."*

"Rena!" came her mother's voice. "When is breakfast?"

"Soon, Mother," she called back and continued singing, *"Oats and toast and grape jelly; oats and toast and grape jelly; Mother dear, don't ever fear; you're soon to taste your oats and toast and grape jelly."*

"And I'm a song writer, too," she told herself merrily as she carried the breakfast tray to her mother.

Rena was soon spooning oatmeal into Addie's mouth. It was becoming simpler just to feed her, as she couldn't handle eating utensils very well any longer. She also needed help with her drinks. She still seemed to enjoy her coffee, although she didn't drink much of her juice.

"Do you want to sit up for a while at the window and watch me work with Suzie Murphy?" she asked when she had washed her mother's face and hands and removed the tray.

"I suppose," her mother said with little enthusiasm.

"Good," Rena said, with more excitement than she felt. "That will make the morning go faster for you if you watch us. Suzie wants to run for rodeo queen this next summer, and I'm going to share some of my riding expertise with her."

"You were a good rider," Addie said tonelessly.

"Thank you, Mother." That's the first compliment you've given me since you told me I'm a good girl, she thought. I'll have to write this down!

About that time Shawn pulled up in the yard with his pickup and horse trailer. A young girl got out and walked around to the back of the trailer to help unload the horse.

Watching the slender girl from the kitchen window, Rena thought how cute she looked. Red-gold hair tumbled down the middle of her back. She moved with the freedom and smoothness of a young antelope as she flung back the clasps on the trailer door. While Rena's eyes evaluated the square shoulders, the straight back, and the slim hips, she corrected her first assessment. "She's not cute, she's beautiful!"

"Who?" Addie asked.

"Shawn's daughter," Rena answered. Suzie had backed a buckskin horse out of the trailer and was now leading him around in a circle. "Her face is as pretty as the rest of her, too. Shawn must be so proud of her."

"Suppose so," Addie said. "Fathers always think their daughters are the cat's meow."

Rena gave her mother a sharp look as she went out the door to join her student. She had time for one thought: She's feeling so depressed. Poor woman.

But all thoughts were concentrated now on Suzie and her horse as she walked out to greet the Murphys. After a brief introduction, Rena examined the horse. "Nice," she said as her eyes scanned his short cannon bone and moved on to his muscular chest and high wither. "This boy should have some speed."

"He does," Suzie said proudly. "We won the quarter horse race at the fair." She put her face close to the horse and looked at him with adoration as she blew in his nostrils. "You beat them all, didn't you, Bucky Boy?" The girl's pert nose was a contrast to the horse's distended nostrils, and her full lips planted a kiss on his soft nose as he surveyed her with warm brown eyes.

"That's a lucky horse," Rena said as she smiled at Suzie's father. "Heaven help you when she starts turning those baby blues on a boy instead of her horse."

"She is a doll, isn't she?" Shawn said. "But she doesn't only look good, she rides good, too." Reaching into the tack box, he pulled out the saddle. "Let's get him saddled, darlin', and show Lorena what you can do."

The next two hours flew by for Rena. She found working with the young rider the most exhilarating thing she had done in a long time. She couldn't remember when she had enjoyed a task so much. Suzie was an enthusiastic learner, and responded to Rena's every suggestion. With the natural riding talent she had, it was obvious the girl would be a picture rider in no time.

Shawn had loaded up Rena's trash in the horse trailer to take to the dump while the lesson was in progress. When he came back, he found teacher and student sitting on the fence discussing the importance of lead changes.

"If you're going in a right circle, your horse should be in a right lead," Rena was explaining.

"I know," Suzie replied, wrinkling her nose. "But sometimes he won't change leads."

"Don't worry. I'll show you how to make him do that," Rena assured the girl.

Shawn walked over and put his arm around his daughter's waist. "Did you learn anything, sweetie?"

"Oh yes!" Suzie said with a giggle. "Rena knows everything about riding. I'm learning so much."

"Well," Shawn said as he measured Rena's long legs encased in tight jeans, "she was a pretty outstanding rodeo queen. You'll never believe this, Lorena, but I wrote a poem about you once as I watched you ride around the arena on that brown horse you called Brandy."

Rena looked embarrassed. "You wrote a poem about me?"

"Yep," Shawn replied as his face turned redder than usual.

"Do you remember the words, Dad," Suzie asked.

"Not all of them," Shawn said quickly. "But I remember one verse." Shawn cleared his throat and recited:

> *"She was a rodeo cowgirl, on her Brandy horse of brown,*
> *Winning all the cowboys' hearts as they rode into town.*
> *She was my rodeo cowgirl going to the rodeo,*
> *And when the points were tallied, boys, the cowgirl*
> *won the show."*

"That's good, Dad," Suzie said admiringly. "I didn't know you could do that."

Shawn looked straight into Rena's blue eyes. "That's me. Always underestimated by you women."

"Why don't you leave Buck here?" Rena said, suddenly changing the subject. "He'll be fine in our pasture, and that will save you loading him up every day."

"Good idea. Are you sure that's all right?"

"I'll check with Boone, but I'm sure it won't be a problem," Rena said. "That way you won't have to worry about the horse, just Suzie."

"And that's enough to worry about," Shawn said as he planted a kiss on his daughter's freckled forehead.

In a few minutes, Rena watched the Murphys pull out of the yard. Suzie was talking excitedly to her father. Shawn looked back at Rena and raised a couple of fingers in goodbye.

"How lucky he is to have that darling girl," Rena said aloud. "And what fun it's going to be working with her."

Rena's thoughts then went back to her childless years with Taylor. She hadn't wanted a baby at first, but later she tried to talk to her husband about having children. "The time isn't right," he always said. "Don't worry me about it now, Rena." Finally she had given up pursuing the issue.

I have missed so much, she thought as she turned toward the house.

As if on cue, Merla and Marla came bouncing out to meet her. Before they could make their demands, Rena said, "Let's build a playhouse, girls."

"We can do it today?" Merla asked in disbelief.

"Today is the day!" Rena said. "Go get your dishes and dolls and we'll build them a house."

It took only a few minutes to push blocks of wood together for beds, chairs, and tables. "Set the table with your dishes, and I'll go bring us some goodies for a tea party," Rena said.

Rena and the girls sat on blocks of wood and enjoyed drinking orange juice from tiny cups while they nibbled on crackers and cookies. She looked at the delighted faces of the children and repeated again, "I have missed so much."

Rena then told the girls to continue playing as long as they wanted, and she went indoors to help her mother back to bed. Addie closed her eyes in sleep immediately, so Rena gathered up the broom and mop and a bucket of water and headed for the back room.

The room wasn't really dirty; it was just dusty from years of non-use. When she finished mopping, she dusted the furniture, and her eyes suddenly noticed the notes she had found in the magazine. She reluctantly picked them up again. "What do I do with them?" she asked herself.

She noticed the date again on the one note. April 15, 1950. Twenty-five years ago. I was twelve years old. I was oblivious to the world then. I had a terrible crush on Matt Walker. That's all I remember about 1950.

Rena laid the notes down hurriedly and picked up her cleaning supplies. She put the broom in a kitchen corner and threw the mop water out the back door. "Couldn't do this in Albuquerque," she said with satisfaction.

After that, Rena rinsed out the mop bucket and hung it on its nail on the back porch. Then she went on out to the woodpile to pick up an armful of wood. The girls had gone home, and the playhouse looked deserted. I need to split some more wood, she told herself.

The wood dropped into the woodbox with more noise than Rena had intended. Don't wake Mother, she admonished herself. She lifted a lid off the range and pushed more wood into its empty fire box. The coals were still red, and the fire immediately leaped to life. Now to think of something to cook for Mother's supper. She doesn't have much appetite anymore, Rena thought.

When Debbie came at seven o'clock to check on her patient, Rena quickly changed into a pair of green slacks and a bright plaid shirt. She ran a comb through her thick hair and brightened her lips with pink lipstick. She found herself anticipating the interlude at the matanza as she picked up her guitar and headed for the car. It's good to get away even for a short while, she thought.

The drive to the old Schwope place took only a few minutes. Rena was amazed at the number of vehicles parked by the house. Young people, older people, and children were scurrying around everywhere. Rena knew none of these people, but she smiled and spoke to them as she carried her guitar toward the house.

A group of men seated on the porch were playing Spanish music on violins and guitars. One guitarist sang in a rich baritone voice and tapped his booted toe to the music. A few couples whirled around on the hard packed dirt in the yard.

A tall, handsome red-head suddenly emerged from a group of people and came over to meet Rena. "You made it!" Shawn said as he reached for her guitar. "Now you can sing for us."

"Are you sure they need any more music?" Rena asked with a smile. "They seem to be doing fine."

"We always need more music," Ernesto said as he walked up. "Go on up to the porch, Rena. Juanito needs a rest. He's been singing a long time."

"Come on," Shawn urged with a smile as he started for the porch.

The Spanish number, *Halisco*, ended, and Juanito jumped up. "I hope you guys are taking over?" he said.

"Yeah, loan me your guitar," Shawn said. "We'll tune up Rena's, and we'll play together." The fiddlers nodded their agreement.

The new guitar duo seconded to the violins for a few pieces while they played traditional Spanish music and a few country western songs. When they started the first bars of the Patsy Cline song, *I Fall to Pieces*, Shawn whispered to Rena, "Sing it."

Rena joined in on the chorus. "*I fall to pieces, each time I see you again. I fall to pieces, time only adds to the pain.*" She went on with the verses, and the yard quickly filled with couples dancing the slow waltz. When the song drew to its poignant ending, there was a moment of silence, and then the singer was saluted with applause and shouts.

"More, more," the crowd chanted.

Rena's face was pink with excitement. She hadn't sung in years, but her love for the music she had played with her father was still just as strong as ever.

"Do you know the song, *Release Me*?" she asked one of the fiddlers.

"What key?" he asked, smiling.

"Key of G," she said happily, and began the first verse.

Several songs followed, and Rena finally said to Shawn, "I shouldn't stay too much longer. I've got to get home, and I don't have much voice left anyway."

"How about doing a yodeling song before you go?" Shawn asked.

Rena smiled and started singing:

> "I want to be a cowboy's sweetheart,
> I want to learn to rope and to ride,
> I want to ride o'er the plains and the desert,
> Out west of the Great Divide,
> I want to hear the coyotes howling
> When the sun sets in the west,
> I want to be a cowboy's sweetheart,
> That's the life I love the best."

The yearning in Rena's voice struck an answering chord in the heart of each listener. All of them had their dreams, and many had felt the pangs of unrequited love.

Rena lowered her head when she finished the song. "It was beautiful," Shawn said softly as he gently wiped away her tears.

"Oh Shawn," Rena said as his intense brown eyes held her teary gaze for a long moment.

"I understand, darlin'."

At that moment Ernesto tapped Rena on the shoulder. "There is someone here to see you. A man standing out there near the fire says he wants to see Rena Brooks."

Rena was confused. "What . . . who . . . ?" she stammered.

"Give me your guitar, Rena," Shawn said with authority. "I'll see you later." Rena stood up and paused uncertainly. "He's standing over there by the fire," Shawn continued. "Go see what he wants."

Rena moved in the direction Shawn pointed, but she had no idea who was waiting for her. Darkness was starting to chase the bright sunlight of the fall evening over the mesas as she took hesitant steps in the direction of the fire.

A figure disengaged itself from the people around the fire and moved toward Rena. She recognized the rhythm of the arms and legs immediately.

"My God! she whispered under her breath. "Taylor!"

Taylor strode swiftly to Rena, stopping in front of her. "Hello, Rena," he said in his swift staccato manner of speaking. "You weren't at home. What are you doing here?"

"Well," Rena hesitated as she put her hands out helplessly. "They're having a matanza, as you can see, and I've been singing."

"So I heard," Taylor said. "Do you suppose you could leave your matanza," Taylor paused slightly as he said the word with distaste, "and come with me? I need to talk to you."

Rena looked around helplessly again. At that moment, Shawn walked up carrying her guitar. "Thanks, Shawn," she said, feeling grateful for his presence.

"I'll put it in your car," Shawn said easily. "You'll probably be leaving soon anyway."

"Yes," Rena said. "I'll be leaving soon."

As Shawn walked away, Taylor took Rena's arm and guided her toward his car. They walked in silence, and Rena smiled to herself when Taylor dodged a cowpile in his path. She couldn't imagine manure on his expensive brown oxfords.

As Taylor held the door and Rena slipped onto the leather covered car seat, she felt her composure returning. "When did you get back from Washington?" she asked in an almost normal voice as Taylor sat down next to her.

"A couple of days ago," Taylor answered flatly. "I can't believe how you just left your job and the house and moved out here. After thinking about it, I decided I'd better come down and see what you're up to."

As Rena looked into Taylor's accusing eyes, she suddenly felt both anger and calmness. "I came here to take care of my mother. I told you that."

"I don't find you taking care of your mother," Taylor said.

"Did you find me singing a song?" Rena asked with mock seriousness.

"Forget the stupidity." Taylor said. "I'm in no mood to play games."

"Well, I was singing, and I was enjoying every minute of it. Did you hear my yodeling? Did you like it?"

"You know what I think of that kind of music, Rena."

"Yes," Rena said. "I know what you think of my kind of music, and anything else I like. You have nothing but scorn for me, my roots, and what makes me the way I am. What do you want to talk to me about? Do you want a divorce? Is that why you drove all this way to talk to me?"

"Do you think we have any future?"

"I wish we did," Rena said as she felt the tears coming.

"Let's go get a motel room in Socorro and talk about it," Taylor said. His voice sounded a little softer as he saw her eyes brim.

"I can't leave Mother," Rena said impatiently.

Taylor looked at the woman by his side for a full minute. He wonders why he ever married me, Rena surmised, and I wonder why I ever thought I wanted to marry him.

"Then I might as well go back to Albuquerque," Taylor said.

"I suppose so," Rena said in a choking voice as she got out of the car. The tears were flowing freely now.

"I'll be in touch," Taylor said.

Rena stood watching the big Lincoln pull away. The receding tail lights seemed to hypnotize her.

Suddenly Shawn was by her side. She went straight into his big arms and cradled her head against his broad chest as she sobbed brokenly. "He's gone," she finally said when the tears subsided.

"I guess so," Shawn said as he pulled his shirt tail out of his jeans. "This is one of those times a man should carry a handkerchief."

As Shawn gently wiped her tears away, Rena thought ironically, I'm sure Taylor has a handkerchief in his pocket, but he'd never think of offering it to me.

Standing up straight and taking a big breath, the shaken girl said, "I'm sorry, Shawn. Thanks for the shoulder and the hankie. I'm going home now. By the way, I really enjoyed working with Suzie today. Bring her out next week."

"I'll do that," Shawn said quietly. "I'll call you."

Rena walked blindly away in the direction of her car.

9

RENA DROVE SLOWLY INTO THE YARD and turned the motor off. She rested her head briefly on her hand as waves of hurtful pain engulfed her body. She felt weak and nauseous. But I'm not crying, she thought in surprise.

Rena raised her head and looked out into the blackness. "It's over," she said quietly. Then she opened the door and stepped out into the darkness. "Blast it," she said in a stronger voice, "it's been over for years. Face facts, girl." She slammed the door and walked resolutely toward the house.

Opening the kitchen door quietly, Rena started down the hall to put her guitar away. She glanced in her mother's room. She seemed to be sleeping. But when Rena returned, she heard her mother calling. "Lorena?"

"Yes?" Rena said as she walked into the room.

"Are you alone?" Addie asked.

"Yes."

"Where is Taylor?"

"He's gone back to Albuquerque. How did you know he was here?" Rena asked dully.

"He stopped by the house, and Debbie told him you were over at the party. Things are not too good with you two, are they?"

"No," Rena replied truthfully. Suddenly she wanted to talk to her mother. "Mother, it hasn't been a good marriage for a long time."

"I know," Addie said. "Sometimes women don't marry the right men."

"I don't think I'm very smart with men, Mother."

"You're as smart as any woman." Addie spoke the words with finality. "Be careful, Rena. Don't make a mistake like I did."

Addie's frail hand lay on the blanket, and Rena covered it with her own. No rings, she noticed as she looked at the two hands, but it didn't matter because she was suddenly feeling close to her mother. A question came to her mind, and before she could stop herself the words tumbled out.

"Mother, what happened in 1950?"

Addie's eyes looked straight ahead. "I'm tired," she replied. "I need to sleep."

The spell was broken. Rena removed her hand and kissed her mother lightly on the forehead. "I'll see you in the morning, Mother."

The telephone interrupted Rena's thoughts as she softly closed the bedroom door. "Who could be calling at this hour?" she muttered.

"Hello, doll," came the smooth words over the miles.

Rena instantly recognized the voice. "Hello, Adam," she said. What next? she thought.

"You sound a little tired. How are things going?"

"Things are fine," Rena said in a detached voice. "Where are you?"

"I'm in Phoenix at a medical convention. I just got in from a banquet and thought about you. I wish you were here with me."

This can't go on, Rena told herself. Get things settled with Adam once and for all.

"Adam," Rena said hesitantly, "we need to talk."

"That's what we're doing, love. Talk to me."

"Adam," Rena said in a stronger voice, "my life is very complicated right now. Please don't make it any worse."

"What are you saying?" Adam asked in a wondering voice. "I would never make things bad for you."

"I'm saying it's over, and I really mean that. Please don't call me anymore." There, it's out, Rena thought with relief.

"Rena, you're just tired and upset. Think about what you're saying."

There was a tremor in Adam's usually confident voice.

"I know exactly what I am saying," Rena said. "I do not want to be involved with you any more in any way. This is goodbye, Adam." Rena hung up the phone with a decisive click.

That wasn't so hard to do after all, Rena told herself as she turned from the phone. Thank God that's done! Suddenly she felt as if a heavy load had been lifted from her shoulders. "Thank you, Lord, for helping me do this," she whispered.

Head lights suddenly shone through the kitchen window. Rena opened the door and recognized Shawn's pickup. She wasn't surprised. It seemed right for him to be there with her right now. She knew she needed him. She closed the door behind her and walked swiftly toward his lights.

"Thought you might want to talk," Shawn called out the window. "How are you doin'?"

"Better now that you're here," Rena said. "Come on in and have a cup of coffee."

"Just what I need after too much partying," Shawn said as he eased his long body out of the truck. "Lead me to your kitchen, pretty lady."

As Shawn's muscular arm encircled her waist, she was aware of the rightness of his touch, in spite of the unsettling events of the last hours. She stopped and turned toward him, looking up into his face. "Hold me, Shawn. Just hold me tight."

Rena felt her body pressed close, and she buried her face in the comforting strength of Shawn's broad chest. She was aware of her screaming nerves starting to calm down, and the tightness of her body relaxing. I could stay here forever, she thought.

Shawn's husky voice brought her back to reality. "Let's go in and have that coffee."

"Sure," Rena said quickly. "I'm sorry."

"Nothing to be sorry about, darlin'."

"Sit down," Rena said as they entered the kitchen. "I've got a pot of coffee on the back of the stove. It should be warm. Hopefully it's not too strong."

"Hopefully it is strong," Shawn said with a grin.

Shawn and Rena sat at the table facing each other. Rena put lots of cream and sugar in her drink. "I only like it for the richness and sweetness of it," she explained.

"None of that stuff for me," Shawn said. "I drink it for the coffee itself."

Rena looked at the big man sitting across from her. His red hair fell in curls over his forehead. He looks so naive and vulnerable, she thought. I'm probably the last thing he needs in his life. The phone conversation with Adam suddenly thrust itself into her thoughts. She shook her head and quietly articulated her thoughts. "I'm probably the last thing you need in your life, Shawn."

Shawn took a sip of coffee. "How 'bout you let me make that decision, Lorena."

As Rena looked deep into Shawn's intent eyes, the telephone suddenly rang loudly and urgently. Rena jumped to answer it. "Yes?" she asked quickly, and an anxious frown creased her forehead.

"Rena, it's Debbie," came the answering voice. "I'm at Darlene's. She called when I was at your mother's house. She's in labor, and there's no time to get her to the hospital. Could you come over and help me?"

"Where's Boone?" Rena asked automatically.

"He hasn't come home yet from the Magdalena Ranch. You'd better get yourself right over here."

"I'll be there," Rena said as she put down the receiver and turned to Shawn. "Darlene's in labor. Debbie is with her, and she wants me to come over and help." Rena looked at Shawn helplessly. "I don't know anything about childbirth."

"I'll go with you," Shawn said quickly. "Suzie's with a friend tonight, and you need to stay here with your mother. I've helped cows have their calves. A baby must not be too different."

Rena's clear sense came back to her with the relief she felt. "It would probably be much better for you to be there than me. I'll bring the little girls over here and take care of them."

In a few minutes Rena had Merla and Marla tucked snugly into bed in the back bedroom. They were asleep almost immediately. She then thought she should alert her mother, so she opened her door and looked in.

"Darlene is in labor, Mother. Debbie's with her. There should be a baby before too long. I hate to disturb you, but I thought you'd want to know."

"I wasn't asleep," Addie said, and added, "I 'spose Boone's not here."

"No, but I'm sure Debbie can handle things. Shawn Murphy is helping her."

"Shawn Murphy?" Addie asked with a frown.

"Yes," Rena said firmly. She didn't want to explain how he got involved. "I have the little girls here," she added.

"It may go fast," Addie said, thinking out loud. "This is her third one, and that's the way the others came."

"I'm sure they'll call us when something happens," Rena said.

"Let me know, no matter what time it is," Addie instructed. "I won't be asleep."

"Sure thing, Mother," Rena said as she headed back to the kitchen. She took a magazine and coffee to her mother's comfortable chair by the window and settled in for however long it would take.

Rena finally dozed off but was awakened by Shawn's voice as he came in with Boone.

"Is it over?" Rena asked as she looked sleepily up at the two men.

"I got my boy!" Boone said exultantly. "I've got to tell Mother!"

As Boone headed to the bedroom, Rena turned to Shawn. "How is Darlene?"

"She's doin' fine," Shawn said with a smile. "She's a good brood mare."

"Shawn," Rena protested.

"Well," Shawn grinned apologetically. "She births babies pretty easy. She'll probably have a dozen before she's done."

Boone came back into the room following that remark. "There won't be that many, Shawn," he said with certainty. "It may be easy for her, but it's pretty hard on me."

Shawn laughed. "Boone arrived right at the end of the delivery. I thought I was going to have to pick him up off the floor. He nearly passed out."

Boone shook his head. "Quite a homecoming," he said as he hurried out the door. "Better get back. Thanks, Shawn. See you all later."

Shawn looked at his watch. "I've got to get home, too. It'll be time to open the store pretty soon."

Rena turned to the window and saw a red glow spreading across the sky above the mountains. "We've got a new day coming, and what's the old saying? 'God's in His heaven; all's well with the world?'"

"Keep believin' that, darlin'," Shawn said as he headed out the door.

Rena turned to go to her mother's room. Addie lay still with her eyes closed, but Rena knew she was awake. "Isn't it wonderful that Boone has a boy," she said softly.

"Yes," Addie said quietly. "Boone has his boy. He named him Rudolph Boone Steiner." She sighed and added, "I don't have to wait any longer now."

One comes, one goes, Rena thought sadly as the tears stung her eyelids. "Don't say that, Mother," she said firmly. "You've got to help us take care of that baby."

Addie didn't reply, and Rena turned away. I'll get a little rest, she thought, before the girls wake up wanting breakfast.

10

RENA WAS FEEDING MERLA AND MARLA cereal and toast on Sunday morning when Debbie knocked at the door. She came in apologizing for being late.

"Sorry," she said shaking her head to clear her bleary eyes. "The party went on pretty late last night, and I overslept."

"Do you want some coffee?" Rena quickly asked.

"Yes, please. Dear Jesus, my poor head." Debbie sat down and put her fingers to her forehead. "I drank too much of Tio Pablo's wine."

"His wine has a reputation for being very good," Rena said as she poured the coffee.

"It's very potent, I can tell you that," Debbie said with a groan.

The little girls sat on the other side of the table with big eyes. "Is you thick, Debbie?" Marla asked.

"I think she is sick," Merla said in a sympathizing voice.

"I'll feel better soon," Debbie assured the girls. "These matanza festivities are too much for me."

"What is a 'tanza?" Marla asked in puzzlement.

"It's a celebration--a party," Rena explained.

"Like a birthday party?" Merla asked.

"Kind of," Rena answered, smiling at the little girls.

As Debbie drank her coffee and talked to the girls, the stress lines on her face lessened. She finally set the mug down and looked over at Rena. "How about you?" she asked with concern. "How do you feel this morning?"

"So-so," Rena said without meeting her gaze.

After a short silence Debbie pursued her questioning. "Who was your visitor? I didn't have time to ask you last night with everything that happened."

"It was Taylor," she said tonelessly and mouthed over the girls' heads, "my husband."

"He didn't stay, I see," Debbie said.

"No," Rena said shortly, and the tone of her voice let Debbie know she shouldn't ask any further questions.

Debbie took the hint and stood up. "Well, I'll take care of Mrs. Steiner. Does she know she has a new grandson?"

"Yes," Rena said with a lilt to her voice. "And she's very happy. The girls and I will go over and check on Darlene and the baby while you're here with Mother." She had told Merla and Marla when they woke up that they had a new baby brother.

"I'll be over later when I finish up here," Debbie called from the bedroom.

The girls were full of excited chatter as they headed home."Does we weally has a baby bruvver?" Marla asked.

"Aunt Rena said we do," Merla said to her sister. "She wouldn't lie to us."

"You're right, Merla," Rena said. "I wouldn't tell a fib about something so important. You're going to be pleased to see him. His name is Rudy. He's named for your grandfather."

The girls tried to digest this news and were silent as they soon stood looking in awe at the new baby. "He's so little," Merla said as she carefully touched his tiny hand.

"Him's so cute," Marla said, smiling broadly.

Boone held his new son carefully as his long legs protruded awkwardly from the rocking chair. Darlene rested in bed with her eyes closed. "Mommy is tired, girls. You can stay here only a little while, and then you must go back home with Aunt Rena." The new father raised his eyes to his sister for her approval. Rena nodded her agreement. Both girls squealed in delight at the prospect of going back home with their aunt.

"You can have fun in the playhouse all day, girls," Rena told them.

"What do you think, Lorena?" Boone asked with a note of pride in his voice. "Does he look like his old man?"

Rena really couldn't tell who the tiny red piece of humanity resembled. "He's a handsome boy," she assured his father.

"He'll be helping me with the ranch chores one of these days," Boone said, smiling.

"I'm sure he will." Rena knew this was the natural progression of a ranch boy. "We've got a male now to carry on the Steiner name and care for the Steiner Ranch."

"You bet!" Boone said.

"The girls and I will take turns holding him if you have anything you need to do right now," Rena offered.

"Sure thing," Boone replied as he handed the tiny bundle to his sister. "I need to check the water in the east pasture where I have some bulls. And I'm taking this week off to stay home and help Darlene with the kids until she feels better."

"That's a good idea," Rena said, obvious surprise in her voice.

"Got to get acquainted with this boy," Boone said as he gave his son a last gentle pat with his big hand.

Rena supervised the two big sisters while they held their little brother. "This is it," Darlene said unexpectedly. "Now that Boone has his boy I'm calling it quits on having babies."

"Well, I don't guess I'm surprised," Rena replied. "This wasn't exactly the easiest way to bring a baby into the world."

"Thank God for Debbie," Darlene said with a sigh. "I hope she's not too tired this morning."

Rena smiled. "You probably feel better than she does. I think after the baby came she went back to the party and celebrated a little too much. But I gave her some coffee, and she's perking better now."

Darlene laughed. "That was a little different kind of celebration than I had!"

"She'll be here soon to check on you," Rena said as she put the baby back in his mother's arms.

At that moment, Debbie appeared and Rena and the two girls got ready to leave. "Get your dolls and dishes so you can play house," Rena said to the girls.

"I wish we could have a party," Merla said as they headed back to Rena's house.

"I want a party, " Marla started chanting. "Party, party, party."

"Well, you girls are going to have to build a ball room," Rena remarked. "Fix yourselves a big room with the wood blocks, and we'll have that party."

The excited children immediately started on their building project, and Rena went into the house to check on her mother. She noticed how pale Addie looked as she lay still and unmoving in her bed.

"The new babe is fine," Rena told her mother. "Debbie's with Darlene now. Merla and Marla are outside working on their playhouse. I've told them they can have their own party today. I'll make them some refreshments. We'll have to celebrate the birth of this new little brother."

Addie nodded her head, and a slight smile crossed her face.

Rena then went to the kitchen and cleaned up the breakfast dishes. I'll put a roast on and also a pot of pinto beans, she told herself. That will be our Sunday dinner and I'll make some broth soup for Darlene. That should make her feel stronger.

After she had things going smoothly in the kitchen, Rena headed for the living room and picked up the guitar. She strummed a while and sang a few hymns. She hadn't sung a hymn in years, but after all, it is Sunday, she thought.

Rena started with *The Old Rugged Cross* and sang a few verses of other favorites. When she finally put the guitar away and walked back down the hall toward the kitchen, her mother motioned to her as she passed her door. "Do you need something, Mother?" she asked cheerfully.

"Sing to me," her mother said. "Bring the guitar and sing."

Rena was surprised. Her mother had never seemed interested in the music she and her father played.

She found herself a little embarrassed as she sat down in her mother's bedroom with the guitar over her lap. "What do you want to hear?" she asked uncertainly.

"Anything," Addie said as she closed her eyes.

Suddenly the words of a song came into Rena's mind:

> *"It is no secret what God can do,*
> *What he's done for others,*
> *He'll do for you.*
> *With arms wide open he'll pardon you,*
> *It is no secret what God can do."*

Rena stopped singing for a moment and looked at her mother. It didn't appear that she was listening, but Addie opened her eyes and raised her hand. "Go on," she said.

> *"There is no night for in His light*
> *You never walk alone,*
> *Always feel at home*
> *Wherever you may roam,*
> *There is no power can conquer you*
> *While God is on your side,*
> *Take him at his promise,*
> *Don't run away and hide."*

Then she repeated the chorus. When she finished the last line, she looked quietly at her mother for a moment. "You know that's true, Mother. It really is no secret what God can do."

Addie nodded her head slightly. "Do you think He forgives us, Lorena?"

"The Bible tells us He forgives us many times over, Mother. All we have to do is repent and ask for His forgiveness."

Rena looked at her mother, so pale and withdrawn. She's starting to leave us, she thought sadly, and she knew she had to ask the question. "Mother, shall we have a prayer and ask for God's forgiveness?"

Addie nodded her head, only slightly.

Rena seldom prayed out loud. She always talked to God silently. She felt awkward as she struggled for words which she knew were important at this time.

"Dear God," she began, "we come to you on this Sunday to tell you we love you, and we want you to be with us. We thank you so much for the beautiful little baby you gave us last night. We ask you to always be with him, keeping him strong as we help him walk in your ways. We know that we need your help in all that we say and do. We also know, Lord, that we have not done all that we should do. We know we have sinned many times. And we are sorry, and we ask your forgiveness. We ask you to be with us, leading and guiding in all we say and do, because we want to be with you forever, dear Lord."

Rena hesitated a moment and then started the Lord's Prayer. She took her mother's hand and saw the pale lips mouth the words with her. When she said, "Amen," she squeezed her mother's hand gently.

Rena felt a peacefulness enfold her being as she said softly to her mother, "God heard us, Mother. He will forgive us, and He will take care of us. Go to sleep and rest, Mother. God is with you."

Addie briefly opened her eyes and whispered. "You are a good girl, Lorena. Thank you."

Rena looked quickly at her mother's chest, but she seemed to be breathing steadily, so she said softly, "I'm going out to the playhouse to have a party with the girls now. We'll be singing some songs. You may be able to hear some of them." She bent down and kissed her mother's soft cheek. "I love you, Mother."

Rena felt reluctant to leave her mother's bedside, but she knew the little girls would come bursting in at any moment, so she tiptoed silently out of the room carrying her guitar.

"Are you ready for the party, girls?" she asked as she approached the playhouse.

"Yes," the two voices chorused cheerily.

"We are weddy," Marla said excitedly. "See our dance woom?"

Blocks of wood were spread in a wobbly rectangle. "What a big ballroom!" Rena said in a pleased voice. "Oh, we have lots of room to dance!"

Rena then played the guitar and sang the songs she remembered that she loved from her childhood. She started with the nursery rhymes and went on into *Looby Loo* and *London Bridge* and *Ring Around the Roses*. The girls danced energetically around the wood pile.

"Now let's sing one for Grandma," Rena suggested. "I think she would like *Twinkle, Twinkle Little Star*. Sing it nice and loud so she can hear it."

The girls sang the song loudly, if not melodiously, and then fell to the ground giggling. Rena took her guitar in the house and put it away. As she glanced in her mother's bedroom she noticed that her patient appeared to be resting quietly. Then she made a pitcher of juice and put some ginger snaps on a plate for party refreshments.

As Rena set the treats down on a large wood block, Debbie came over from Boone's house. "Want to join our party?" Rena asked with a grin.

"No thanks," Debbie said. "I've had enough parties for a while. I'll just check on your mom one more time."

The girls quickly settled down to their goodies, and Rena went back in the house. Debbie was taking her mother's pulse, a concerned look on her face.

"How's she doing?" Rena asked

Debbie didn't answer. She kept her finger on Addie's wrist and studied her watch. Then she carefully put the thin hand down.

Debbie put her arm around Rena's shoulders. "Her pulse is weak," she said softly. "I think she has gone into a coma."

"What does that mean?" Rena asked sharply.

"She's going to her heavenly home soon," Debbie replied with compassion in her voice.

"How long?"

"A few hours, probably. It's hard to tell for sure, but it won't be long. I'll take the girls home and tell Boone and Darlene."

After Debbie left, Rena stood as if transfixed while deep sobs fought their way out of her body. "Oh no," she said over and over. Even in that wrenching moment she knew the tragic thing about it all was not that her mother was dying. She cried because they had known so little closeness in all their years together.

Rena went in the bedroom and looked down at her mother's still pale face. She gently took one of the limp hands in her own while trying to stifle the hurtful moans of pain and despair which struggled to escape from deep within her soul.

It took a while to fully realize her brother was beside her, supporting her with his quiet strength. "It's best, Lorena. She didn't want to live anymore. You did a good job taking care of her."

I really gave her so little, Rena's broken heart cried.

11

RENA FELT LIKE A ROBOT during the next week as she performed the necessary duties of a bereaved daughter. Her world seemed dark and surreal. It will all go away soon, she told herself.

"We need to meet with the funeral director and make the arrangements," Boone had told her, and she went dutifully with him and sat and stared at the quiet soft spoken man as he droned on. She heard nothing he said. Mother would hate this, she thought.

They followed the director into a back room to look at caskets. But she could only look over the top of them. "How about this one?" Boone asked, pointing to an oak box.

"That's fine," Rena said as she turned and left the room.

Back in the director's office, they were presented with a paper of figures. Rena glanced at the bottom line and thought, Mother would never spend that much money. Later she didn't remember what the figure was.

The only thing she remembered vividly about that scene was the picture of a red rose the director had showed them. "This could be put on the inside of the lid of the casket over your mother's face," he softly said. "The extra cost would be twenty-five dollars."

Boone had looked at Rena. For the first time Rena said what she thought. "No!" she said vehemently. She knew that picture would cost two dollars in any dime store. Boone was looking at her strangely. "I'm sorry," she said in a strained voice. "Mother wouldn't like that."

"Very well," the director said. "Then everything is settled. The service will be on Wednesday at the funeral home. We'll set it at two o'clock in the afternoon. Do you want me to take care of the music?"

"No," Rena said in a clear voice. "There will be one song, and I'll sing it."

"That will be nice. And what is the name of the song, please?"

He's trying to be patient with me, Rena realized. "*It is No Secret What God Can Do*, at the very end of the service." She added, "Please."

"Of course. That will be nice."

If he says how nice things are again, I'll scream, Rena thought. She had never felt so thankful to breathe fresh air as when they stepped out the door of the funeral home.

"I'm glad you're singin' for Mother," Boone said as they drove away.

"I'm not sure I can do it, but I'm going to try," Rena said. "I know she liked that song."

"You can do it," Boone said encouragingly. "You're a very strong person, Rena."

I wish, Rena thought.

Then there were endless phone calls and visits from friends and neighbors. Somehow Rena got through all of it, saying little except, "Thank you." "Thank you." "Thank you."

Food streamed into the house, and Rena filled the refrigerator and the deep freeze. She knew people would gather after the funeral, so all the salads and cakes and rolls and casseroles would come in handy then.

Of the endless string of people who found their way in and out of the house, the only ones Rena remembered were Suzie and Shawn. Suzie carried a cake she had made. "She's a good cake maker," Shawn said.

"I'll be sure to eat some of it," Rena said, but the thought of it turned her stomach. She couldn't imagine ever being hungry again.

Later that day Suzie went to ride her horse for a while, and Shawn took Rena's arm and led her down a grassy trail toward the bosque. "You need a little fresh air," he said, and Rena went with him, thankful for the distraction.

They walked through the vineyard in silence and then stopped under the shade of a large grove of tamaracks that grew near the water. Shawn noticed that the pinkish lavender branches framed Rena's blonde beauty to perfection. He put his hands on Rena's waist and looked deeply into her eyes. "How are you doin'?" he asked tenderly.

"There's a lot to cope with right now," Rena said in a small voice.

"I know," Shawn whispered as he drew her into his arms. "You know I want to help, Lorena."

"I know," Rena said as she buried her face in his soft leather jacket. She couldn't hold back the tears that ran down her cheeks. Shawn said nothing as he stroked her hair gently.

Finally, Rena pulled her face back and wiped her eyes. "Now you've got a big tear stain on your jacket."

"That's all right," Shawn said. "That jacket couldn't have sweeter tears on it. Do you feel a little better?"

"I guess so," Rena answered as she tried to smile. "What would I do without your shoulder to cry on once in a while? You're a good friend, Shawn."

Shawn put his hand under Rena's chin and raised her face. "This probably isn't the time to say this, but I'm hoping to be more than a friend to you, Rena."

Rena looked deep into the brown eyes gazing longingly into hers. She knew she couldn't give him the response he wanted at this time. "I'd better get back to the house," she said apologetically.

Shawn silently led the way up the trail to the pasture where Suzie was riding. They stopped to watch the little cowgirl for a few minutes before Rena turned toward the house. "See you later?" Shawn called to her retreating figure.

Rena turned around. "Sit by me at the funeral?"

"You bet!" Shawn answered with a smile.

The next day Rena heard nothing the minister said at the funeral. She knew the words didn't apply to her mother anyway, and she sat thinking her own thoughts. Her heart ached as she tried to fatham this person who was being eulogized. I'm her own daughter, and I didn't know her. How could you possibly know anything about her? she thought as the speaker droned on.

The song was the only meaningful part of the service to Rena. She sang it with all the emotion in her broken heart. She closed her eyes, and when she sang the words, *with arms wide open, He'll pardon you*, she knew that her mother was resting safe in the arms of her God. When she bowed her head at the end of the song, she was repeating the words to herself, *it is no secret what God can do.* She went back to sit down between Shawn and Suzie, and she knew her mother would be pleased with the song. For the first time in many months, she actually felt at peace with herself.

After everything was over, Rena looked around the empty rooms of her mother's home. Her bed looked sterile and cold without the slight figure under the covers. Her easy chair at the kitchen window looked lonely and forbidding. She knew she would never sit in that chair again.

"Dear God, what am I going to do?" she said out loud. She heard the spoken words and really didn't know who had said them. She only knew she had never felt so lost and alone.

Suddenly the telephone rang, and Rena tried to collect her thoughts. She lifted the receiver tentatively and said in a low voice, "Hello."

A confident male voice answered. "Rena Brooks?"

"Yes." Rena didn't recognize the voice.

"This is Paul Sanchez. I was your mother's attorney. Would you and your brother be able to come into my office tomorrow morning so we can start the wheels moving on settling the estate?"

"The estate?" Rena asked blankly.

"Yes," the confident voice continued. "We'll read your mother's will and go to the probate judge."

"All right," Rena replied. "What time?"

"How about ten o'clock?"

"That's fine."

"Good. I'll call your brother about this meeting as well."

After Rena hung up, she thought, well at least I know what I'll be doing tomorrow. She was aware that her life seemed to have no focus now that her mother was gone.

"Maybe I should call Taylor," she murmured as she stood in the middle of the kitchen. She hadn't wanted him to think he would have to come to the funeral, so she hadn't called him about her mother's death.

Now she could call the house in Albuquerque and just leave a message about the funeral today.

Rena was surprised when the phone was immediately answered. "Hello," came Taylor's familiar voice.

"Oh, you're home," Rena said uncertainly.

"Yes, I am. How are you, Rena? Your voice sounds a little different. Is everything all right?"

"Well, I guess so," Rena said haltingly. "Well, not really. We buried Mother today."

"Your mother died?" The question exploded over the wires. "And you didn't tell me?" Taylor asked with anger in his voice.

Rena didn't really know what to say. "Well . . . "

"When did this happen?" the demanding voice pursued.

Rena swallowed and tried to get control of her thoughts and her voice. "She died on Sunday."

Taylor hesitated. "Well I'm sorry, Rena. But why didn't you call me?"

"I don't really know," Rena said honestly. "I thought you probably weren't there, and if you were, you wouldn't want to come. I guess that's what I thought."

"Rena, we've got to talk," Taylor said, his voice sounding very tired and discouraged.

"Later," Rena said quickly. "I'm very busy now. I have to meet with Mother's lawyer tomorrow."

"I'll be in touch with you later in the week," Taylor said. "We'll arrange a meeting. I'm not going back east for a while."

Rena suddenly felt no strength left in her body. "All right," she said tiredly. "Must go now. Bye." She walked down the hall and threw herself on the couch. "I should have called him," she said out loud. "I just can't do anything right." The restless nights since her mother had died suddenly caught up with her, and she fell into a troubled sleep.

12

PAUL SANCHEZ SMILED BROADLY as he extended his hand to Rena and said, "It's been a pleasure, my dear. Again, my sincere regrets over your loss. But everything is in order and the legal steps will be taken to make you and your brother the sole recipients of the estate and all its assets. As I said, your father set up this trust before he died. He wanted to assure his children of their inheritance."

Rena suddenly felt overwhelmed with legalities and legal people. Earlier they had met with the probate judge, and their lawyer had presented him with the necessary papers to begin to probate the will.

"Thank you, sir," Rena said, and she and Boone headed for the door.

"Let's have lunch," Boone said. "You look like you need something in your stomach, and I know I do."

Rena walked blindly down the main street of Socorro with her brother and automatically stepped through the door he held open. The strong smell of food met her nostrils, and she felt nauseated. "I'm not very hungry," she said uneasily.

"Maybe you could eat a bowl of soup," Boone said. "Mary, the cook here, makes delicious rolls and soup."

Rena glanced around nervously and located an arrow that pointed toward the restrooms. "I'll go wash my hands," she said hastily.

Rena made the haven of the restroom and crouched over the stool as dry heaves gripped her body. There wasn't anything to come up since she had eaten nothing that morning before Boone came by for her. A few minutes later, Rena rose shakily to her feet and splashed cold water on her eyes and face. That's good, she thought. Maybe I'll feel better now.

"Are you all right?" Boone asked when she returned.

"Sure," Rena replied.

"You're awfully white," Boone said, with obvious concern.

"It's just nerves," Rena replied with a frown.

Boone put his large calloused hand over Rena's small trembling one that lay on the table. "It's going to be all right, Sis. You've been through a bad time, taking care of Mother like you did. I know it was tough, but you did a good job."

"Thanks," Rena said with a sigh. "I wish I could have done more for her."

"There wasn't much more that could have been done," Boone said. "She got to come home and die where she wanted to be. I know that meant a lot to her."

At that moment the waitress set large bowls of tempting smelling soup in front of them. "It looks like Mother's beef soup," Rena noted with a little interest.

"And these are home-made rolls," Boone said with enthusiasm. "Butter one of them up, and you've got a lunch here fit for the Queen of England."

They ate in silence for a few minutes, and Rena soon realized the warm liquid in her stomach did make her feel better. She looked across the table at Boone and said with a half-smile, "This is a delicious lunch. Thanks for bringing me."

"Finish your roll," Boone directed. "Mind your big brother."

Rena put more butter on her roll and looked around the café with interest. There weren't too many customers at this time of day. A couple of men sat at the counter eating silently, and another sat at a table by himself not too far from them. Her eyes met his, and he smiled. Rena smiled back. I guess I'm supposed to know him, she thought as she looked away.

Boone soon pushed aside his empty soup bowl and motioned to the waitress. "Piece of apple pie, please ma'am. Make it two."

"Oh, no," Rena said. "I couldn't."

"Sure you can," Boone said. "Mary's pie is the best. A cup of coffee and a piece of pie will be just what the doctor ordered."

Rena was surprised at how good the pie tasted with the coffee. She felt her taut nerves relaxing, and she looked around the room again and noticed the eyes of the same man were still on her. "I wonder who he is," she said aloud.

"Who?" Boone asked as he pushed a large bite of pie into his mouth. He followed Rena's eyes. "Never saw him before," he answered nonchalantly.

Putting aside her curiosity about the man in question, Rena's thoughts then returned to the meeting they had attended earlier. She felt there was something she needed to say to Boone regarding the estate. "Boone," she said slowly, "I have never paid any attention to the ranch business. I guess I really never knew it was such a big operation. You're the one who has always been here and worked on the ranch. I'm sure you deserve much more of it than I do."

"Of course I don't," Boone said firmly. "You're the daughter of Rudy and Adelheid Steiner, and you are an equal heir with the son. The way the trust is set up, I will continue to manage the ranch and will be paid accordingly for my work. But you also will receive a monthly sum as half owner. It won't be as much as mine, but you won't do as much work as me, either."

Rena shook her head as if to clear away the cobwebs in her brain. "I don't think I deserve anything."

Boone laughed. "What would Dad say about that? You were his very favorite girl, you know. I'm surprised he didn't want you to have the whole ranch."

"He was a very fair man, Boone," Rena said indignantly.

Boone's face turned serious and he said earnestly, "Yes, he was, Rena. And I hope to be half the man he was."

A voice suddenly interrupted their conversation. Rena looked up to see the man who had been staring at her. "Excuse me," he said pleasantly.

Boone glanced up. "Yes sir. Can we help you?"

"I'm William Estes," the man said as he held out his hand. "I'm visiting in town. I worked in this area years ago, and I couldn't help but notice how much the lady resembles someone I knew then."

Boone took the man's hand and said jovially, "Well, she must have been a beautiful lady then. I'm Boone Steiner, and this is my sister, Lorena."

Rena looked into the direct blue eyes of the older man who stood tall and straight. A shock of white hair was combed back in a deep wave. He was dressed in an expensive western jacket with a turquoise bolo around his neck. What a nice looking man, Rena thought as she shook his hand. He looks familiar.

"You are Steiners?" their new friend asked with a note of excitement in his voice. "I worked on the Steiner Ranch when I was here. I worked for Rudy and Addie Steiner."

"That's our father and mother," Boone said quietly.

"I knew there was some connection when I looked at you." William Estes looked straight at Rena and addressed her. "You look very much like your mother. She was, as your brother says, a beautiful lady."

Rena felt confused. No one had ever told her she looked like her mother, and she had never really wanted to look like her. "Oh?" she said, as lines of puzzlement creased between her eyes.

"Yes," the man continued. "The same eyes and hair. Forgive my staring at you. When you walked in the room, you were like a page from my past." The man's face was shining with pleasure, and there was a hint of a tear at the corner of one eye. "This is such good luck to find you two here." He continued to stare at Rena, and her eyes were locked into his gaze.

"When did you work for my parents, Mr. Estes?" Boone's voice broke the spell of the strange moment.

"Call me Will," the man said, turning to Boone with an effort. "It was a long time ago. I entered college that fall with the money I had saved. I went down to Texas A and M and got an engineering degree and then went to work in Houston for a large oil company. I've worked for the same company for many years. When I was invited to do a little speaking here at the college, I thought it would be interesting to come back to this place where I had worked so long ago." Will turned his attention back to Rena. "I remember you as a little whippersnapper with long legs and pigtails. There was only the one child then."

"I wasn't born until nineteen-fifty," Boone said. "She's my big sister." He smiled at Rena affectionately.

"And how are your parents?" Will asked, addressing Boone.

"Not here anymore," Boone replied. "Dad's been gone for many years, and we just buried Mother yesterday."

"Oh, I'm sorry," Will said. "I didn't know." There was obvious concern on his face.

"No way you could've known," Boone said.

"That's right," their new friend replied. "But I've taken up too much of your time." He suddenly seemed distracted and started to turn and walk away.

"It's nice to meet you," Boone said. "You're welcome to come out to the ranch and visit us while you're here."

"Thank you. I'm going to be very busy. I'm here to try to influence some young men to become petroleum engineers. We're going to need many of them in Houston."

"Good luck," Boone said with a smile. "Just don't try to influence my son in that direction in about twenty years. He's going to be taking over the Steiner Ranch."

"I promise I won't do that," Will said with a smile as he walked away.

Rena was very quiet on the way back to the ranch. She was thinking about the man they had met. Many men had worked on the ranch as she grew up. She had paid little attention to any of them. She didn't remember this one; yet seeing him today had certainly aroused her interest.

Boone's voice interrupted her thoughts. "I don't know what your plans are, Rena, but I want you to know you can stay in Mother's house as long as you like--forever would be great. The girls are so happy having a real aunt close by. I don't know what your situation is with Taylor, but it's as plain as the nose on your face there are problems there. I don't want to pry, but maybe the ranch is just what you need right now."

"You're right, there are problems," Rena said. "And I really don't know what I'll be doing, but it would be nice to stay here while I try to figure things out."

"I'll help you any way I can," Boone said. "Just let me know if you need anything."

"Thank you," Rena said. "It's nice to have a big brother around." She looked over gratefully at her sibling. His intent blue eyes returned her gaze. Suddenly she knew why she had thought William Estes looked familiar. Boone had eyes just like him.

13 ～～～～～～～～～～～～～～～～～～～～～～～～～

"I SHOULD CALL TAYLOR," Rena said to the quiet walls as she wandered around in the silent house. But instead of picking up the telephone, she went into the living room and lay down on the couch. Suddenly she felt very tired. I'm exhausted, she thought as she closed her eyes.

Rena was aroused by the insistent ringing of the telephone. She pulled herself up with an effort and shuffled to the kitchen. "Hello," she said sleepily.

"Did I wake you?" Shawn's voice said crisply. "I've tried to call you several times. I was about ready to call Boone and have him check on you."

"I was just taking a nap," Rena said as she stifled a yawn. "I seem to be very tired. Sorry I didn't hear you."

"No problem, just as long as you're all right," Shawn said cheerily.

Rena's mind came back into focus. "We met with the lawyer this morning," she said. "It was a grueling session, but necessary, of course. I guess now I own half of a ranch."

"You should have known that," Shawn said.

"I just hadn't thought about it. You'll have to tell me what to do with my part of the rancho," she said, laughing.

"I'm sure Boone will have all that figured out," Shawn said quickly. "But I'll give you an idea. Suzie has a friend who wants to come out with her when she rides tomorrow. She's interested in riding lessons, too. Maybe you should start a riding school."

"That would be fun," Rena said. "I'll think about your idea. But first I've got a lot of loose ends to tie up."

"I know," Shawn said. "I'd like to help you, but I don't want to intrude. Just let me know when you need me. I can't come out tonight because I have a city council meeting. We have sewer lines that need dug up and replaced, so we have big decisions to make. You probably just need to rest anyway."

"I think so," Rena agreed. On the spur of the moment she added, "Shawn, I met a gentleman in town today who I found quite interesting. He's an engineer from Houston, and he's lecturing at the college for a few days. He says he worked for my parents years ago before he went to college. I'd kind of like to talk to him about what he remembers about them. Could you keep an eye out for him and maybe bring him along with you and Suzie when you come out tomorrow? I've got a lot of food left over from the funeral dinner. I could fix supper for us."

"I've noticed a stranger in the café. Is he a tall nice looking older man?" Shawn asked, as if thinking aloud.

"Yes," Rena said. "He dresses in western apparel. He has white hair and very blue eyes."

"What's his name?"

"William Estes. He told us to call him Will."

"William Estes. Will," Shawn said thoughtfully. "You know, I've heard the old timers talk about a good bronc rider named Billy Estes who worked for your folks. Could that be the same man?"

"I wonder," Rena said, and then thoughtfully added, "Billy, Will, that sounds very much like the same name."

"I tell you what," Shawn said. "I'll make it a point to introduce myself to this fellow and try to bring him out to the ranch tomorrow."

"Good!" Rena said in a pleased voice. "I'll fix supper for us after the lesson. We'll show him a little Socorro hospitality and get acquainted with him in the process."

"Maybe he can give the teacher some riding tips," Shawn said, teasing her.

"No doubt he can if he's who we think he is," Rena replied, laughing.

"All right, it's settled then. We'll be out after school tomorrow about four thirty."

"It's a date."

Rena put the phone down with a smile on her face. Then her eyes narrowed, and she said aloud, "I've got to find out just what your relationship was with my mother, Mr. Estes."

Rena was completely awake now, and she rummaged in the refrigerator for a supper snack. She decided on a bowl of fruit salad and a glass of milk. "I'll have the ham tomorrow for my company," she whispered, "along with baked potatoes." Food suddenly sounded good to her so she took out a peach pie for her dessert.

Boone came to the door while she was eating. "Just thought I'd check on you," he said with a smile.

"Come on in," Rena replied. He's trying to be a good brother, she thought, and he hasn't had much practice at it. "I'm having my supper. Do you want to join me?" Rena asked.

"Well, I just ate, but a piece of pie would taste mighty good," Boone said.

"Rena cut a generous slice of the dessert for her brother and poured him a glass of milk. "Sorry I don't have anything else to drink," she said. "I'm trying to cut down on the coffee. I've been drinking too much of it lately."

"Milk will be just fine," Boone assured her.

"How's the baby?" Rena asked between bites.

"Doin' good," Boone answered. "You should see him eat. All he does is eat and sleep and fill his pants."

At that moment Rena looked straight into Boone's eyes. The light was behind his head and she couldn't see their color plainly. As she searched his eyes, she asked nonchalantly, "Boone, did you ever hear Daddy speak of a bronc rider named Billy Estes?"

Boone chewed his bite of pie and thought for a few moments. "Billy Estes," he said slowly. "Billy Estes. That name does sound familiar. Why?"

"Well, you know we met that man today who said his name is Will Estes. He said he worked for Daddy. Shawn tells me he thinks there was a bronc rider who worked on the ranch whose name was Billy Estes. I'm wondering if it could be the same man."

"Might be," Boone said as he pushed his chair back. "That was good pie. Well, I'd better get back and check on Darlene and the baby."

What a good family man he's becoming, Rena thought. "Thanks for stopping by," she said. "Tell the girls to come over and see me tomorrow."

"They'll love that," Shawn said, "and I'll love getting them out of my hair. They're quite the little rascals."

"They are dolls," Rena said emphatically as Boone went out the back door.

Rena then cleared the table and put the dishes in the sink. I'll do them tomorrow, she promised herself.

Rena turned from the sink and looked out the big kitchen window. The moon was shining brightly as it came up over the mountains in the east and highlighted the peaceful ranch landscape of trees bordering the river which meandered behind quiet cattle silhouetted in the pasture. The vista gave her a feeling of calmness and rightness. There wasn't a sound to mar the perfect solitude and beauty of the evening. Such a contrast to the lights and noise of her Albuquerque home at this time of night, she thought. "This is the place I love," she realized as she whispered the words. "This is the place I belong."

Rena drank in the beauty of the night for long minutes. Then she turned and walked slowly toward the back bedroom. She switched on the light and looked over at the dresser. The notes that had fallen out of the magazine were still lying there by a jewelry box where she had tossed them.

Slowly Rena unfolded one of the pieces of paper. "See you tomorrow at the same place. Love, B." Nice handwriting, she noted to herself. She carefully picked up the next note. "I'm the luckiest man in the world. See you Saturday. Love, B." Good spelling, she thought. Rena then picked up the third note and squinted her eyes as she read the date, "4-15-50."

"That's the year Boone was born," she said to the face staring back at her from the dresser mirror. "He was born the twenty-seventh of November."

Rena's eyes went back to the note. "He knows. I must go. Love you always. B." The writing is more scrawled on this note, she told herself. It looks as if it were written in a hurry. Well, maybe it was. Apparently he was leaving fast.

A feeling of guilt suddenly pervaded Rena's thoughts. She hurriedly put the notes in the jewelry box and closed the lid. She stopped by the bathroom and washed her hands as if to wash away the uncomfortable inferences of the notes.

Suddenly Rena felt weary again. I must get to bed, she told herself. She wanted sleep to wipe away all her churning thoughts.

But as she lay in bed, the thoughts persisted. He said my mother was beautiful, she remembered. He said I look like her.

Somehow she had to uncover the whole story. She instinctively suspected that what had happened to her mother had affected their relationship. She had to understand the mystery of her mother's coldness to her. "If I understand her, maybe I can understand myself better," she said with a sigh as fatigue claimed her stressed mind and body, and sleep ruled in spite of her troubled thoughts.

14

RENA SPENT SATURDAY MORNING with Boone and Darlene and the children. She bathed the baby and changed the beds and did some washing. The little girls watched her every movement and chattered constantly.

"Do somethin' with us," Merla asked wishfully.

"Pwease," Marla chimed in.

"All right, girls," Rena said with a sigh as she put the laundry basket down after hanging out the last load of clothes. "I'll empty the wash water, and then we'll make cookies."

"I'll take that water out," Boone said. "You just keep those kids occupied."

In a few minutes, Rena was mixing cookie dough in her bowl and had shown the girls how to do the same thing in another bowl. This is not so simple, Rena soon realized. Their little hands didn't handle big spoons, stirring, and adding ingredients very well. Soon there was flour all over the table, floor, faces, and hair of the cooks. But Rena made the best of it.

"Shall we make cookie kitties?" she asked.

"Yes!" Merla shouted.

"I want wabbits," Marla said as she clapped her hands in delight.

"We can have both," Rena assured the cooks. "Also ponies and turtles. Whatever you want."

Rena put her pan of cookies in the oven to bake and watched the girls create their animals. She gave them raisins to use for eyes and left them to their fun. "Call me when you're ready to put the cookies in the oven," she said as she headed for the bedroom to rock the baby.

"He's growing already," she said to Boone. "He's going to be a big boy. I think he resembles you." She gazed into the baby's big blue eyes and thought, you'll have eyes like your dad and perhaps also like Will Estes.

"Thanks for all your help," Boone said as he sat down in a chair near Rena and the baby. "You know, there's a lot of work around here. I'll be happy to get back to riding the range!"

"We're ready to cook our cookies," Merla interrupted.

"Please put them in the oven for the girls, Boone," Rena said. "My cookies should be ready to come out now."

Boone sighed and clumped into the kitchen in his cowboy boots. "No rest for the wicked," he said in mock misery as he opened the oven door. "Ouch!" he yelled as he burned his hand on the hot pan.

"Are you all right?" Darlene immediately called out in a concerned voice.

"Okay!" Boone shouted as he set the pan down on the counter with a bang and turned to the sink to run cold water over his hand.

"Put hot pads under that pan so it doesn't burn the counter," Rena directed quickly. "And don't burn your hand again!" She took the baby back to his mother and turned her attention to the crisis in the kitchen. After she put the girls' cookies in the oven, Rena opened a cabinet door to look for soda to put on Boone's burned hand. She mixed up a paste of soda and water and told Boone to sit down and put his hand on the table while she covered the burned area with the soothing creamy concoction. "This will make it feel better," she assured her red faced brother.

The girls were squealing for a cookie, so she set them down at the table with cookies and milk while she fixed a treat for Boone and herself. After a few bites Boone was in a better mood. "I guess there are advantages to working in the kitchen," he mumbled as he crunched cookies.

Rena laughed and offered some advice. "Get used to it. These girls are going to be making cookies from now on, right?"

"Yeth!" Marla said as she dropped crumbs all over the table."It'th fun!"

Rena took the second batch of cookies out of the oven and bragged about the wonderful animals the girls had made. It was impossible to tell what some of them were, but she knew they would taste good, and the girls would be so proud of their creations.

"This is the first time I've ever made cookies with little girls," she said thoughtfully. She suddenly realized again how much she had missed by not having had children.

After a while, Rena washed the dishes and pans they had used in their baking and swept up the flour and raisins from the floor. She then put on a pot roast and gave a skeptical Boone instructions as to when to add carrots and potatoes and when to serve the meal. "And remember to use pot holders," she reminded him with a wink.

"I'll be sure to do that," Boone answered seriously.

Poor fellow, Rena thought as she walked back to her house. "But it's good for him," she said to the tabby cat that peered at her cautiously from behind a cottonwood.

Rena then grabbed a broom and started in on her own kitchen. Her company would be here in a couple of hours. She realized she must have everything cleaned and organized before they arrived because she'd be with Suzie most of the time supervising her riding. Rena hummed as she worked. For the first time since her mother had died, she felt her spirits lifting. She looked forward to seeing Suzie and Shawn, but she knew the anticipation she felt was mainly because of Will Estes. "I'm going to put him on the spot," she murmured. "He's going to tell me about my mother."

Rena brought potatoes from the pantry under the kitchen as well as two cans of green beans and a can of mushroom soup. Her menu would be ham, Jello fruit salad, rolls and apple pie, all left over from the funeral dinner, plus baked potatoes and green beans fancied up with mushroom soup and seasoned with a few slices of onion.

After her kitchen chores, Rena changed into jeans and riding boots. She pulled her long honey blonde hair back with a blue ribbon that complimented her eyes. She hadn't really looked at herself in weeks. Personal appearance had not been one of her priorities since she had come home, but now she hesitated before the long mirror in her bedroom and closely inspected the woman who smiled back at her. She tossed her hair back and turned sideways and analyzed her reflection.

"Preening before the mirror again." She could almost hear her mother say those words to her. "You can never walk in front of a mirror without looking at yourself."

It was true, and she had usually approved of what she saw in the mirror. She had been blessed with thick cooperative hair that always looked attractive whether she spent an hour on it or a minute. She liked her long legs, her square shoulders and her ample breasts that rose over slim hips and a small waist. Her blue eyes had a sparkle today, and her lips curved automatically into a smile.

"Not too bad for a thirty-seven year old gal," she commended herself. She then walked with quick sure steps out the door as Shawn's pickup pulled up. She was pleased to see that Will Estes was crowded in with Suzie and her friend.

"It's a good thing I'm fairly thin, or we would never have fit in there," Will said as he got out and smiled at Rena.

Shawn came around the pickup and introduced Suzie's friend. "This is Isabel Carrillo," he said. "Isabel, this is Lorena Brooks. Isabel's father is getting her a new barrel horse, and he's interested in her having riding lessons. She'd like to watch what Suzie does today."

"Nice to have you all," Rena said with a warm smile as they headed for the pasture.

Rena and Isabel stood by the fence as Shawn saddled Suzie's horse. Will had walked off to refresh his memory of the lay of the ranch. In a few minutes he came back and said, "I worked for your dad over in the east pasture where Boone has his bulls now. That's where I broke and trained the horses for the ranch hands."

"Yes," Rena said. "I vaguely remember horses in that pasture." After a moment's hesitation she added, "I hear you were quite a hand with a horse."

Will gazed out over the landscape with a faraway look in his alert blue eyes and nodded. "I broke a lot of 'em, and I rode most of 'em. Once in a while I met one that cleaned my clock."

"You also rodeoed?" Rena asked.

"Yeah. Picked up a buckle every now and then." Will gestured with a humble smile to his middle. A large oval shaped silver buckle graced his belt.

"I'm impressed," Rena said. "By the way, I've been working with Suzie to teach her how to get her horse to shift his lead. She'll be riding the figure eight pattern today. Watch her and see if she gets it right."

"Sure thing," Will said as he held the barbed wire of the fence apart so Rena could get through and walk over to her student.

Shawn came over to the fence and stood by Will and Isabel as Suzie started her pattern. All watched in silence for a while. "How do you think she's doing?" Shawn finally asked Will.

"She's a good natural rider," Will replied. "She sits well in the saddle and has good command of her horse. I can see she's got a good teacher."

"Well, I knew Lorena would be the one to work with her. She was our rodeo queen when she was in high school, and she won first runner up in the state competition. She was an excellent rider. Of course, her dad had her on a horse from the time she could straddle a saddle."

"Yes, I remember her riding," Will said. "I remember her mother complaining that she never did anything in the house because she was always on a horse."

"She loved it," Shawn said. "I came out to ride with her one time. I was a town boy and wasn't much of a rider. I just wanted to be with her. Well, my horse got too close to a wooden fence while we were having a race, and he scraped me off. I had a knee bunged up and lost some skin on one leg. That was the last time I tried to keep up with Lorena on a horse."

"She's like her dad," Will said, chuckling at the story. "He was quite a horseman and loved a good spirited mount. I guess that was his undoing in the end, from what I heard."

"Yeah that's what happened. It was a tough thing for Addie and the kids. Boone was only a little tyke. But he's just like his dad on a horse now. He doesn't ride as much as his dad, though. He hires a helicopter to round up the cattle on the Magdalena Ranch in the spring. But he's a good hand with a horse."

"He seems like a good man, period," Will said.

"He grew up fast," Shawn said. "Circumstances forced him to become a man early in life."

Just then Rena joined them while Suzie continued to ride in figure eight patterns, urging her horse to change into the proper leads. Rena looked at Will and said with a grin, "As an old bronc buster, do you have any hints about training a horse to change leads?"

"What have you told her?" Will asked.

"I've told her what my dad told me. Shift your weight and give him a tug to the side you want him to go to."

"That's basically what you do," Will said. "I also gave my horse a cue when I wanted him to change leads. I pushed my heel gently into the side I wanted him to turn away from, and then I shifted my weight and gave him the tug."

"That sounds worth trying," Rena said as she headed back to her student.

A few minutes later Rena came back. "I'm going to the house to put food on the table," she said. "You can come with me, Isabel. Why don't you two keep an eye on Suzie. See how she does with her lead changes. Come on to the house in about thirty minutes, and I'll have supper ready."

Isabel proved to be a talkative teenager while she and Rena worked in the kitchen. She was excited about getting a new horse and becoming a barrel racer. "I hope you'll work with me the way you've helped Suzie," she said with a shy smile.

"I'm going to think seriously about that," Rena said. "Now get the ham and the rolls out of the warming oven while I take out the baked potatoes and put on the salad and drinks. I'll also pour the green beans into a bowl. They smell so good. I think we have all worked up a good appetite."

Rena was pouring warm water from the teakettle into the wash pan when Suzie, Shawn, and Will trooped in the door.

"Smells good," Suzie said with a dimpled smile. "I'm so hungry! And we're changing leads better, you'll be happy to know."

"Wash your hands and sit down before the food gets cold," Rena said with a smile. "And I'm happy about the leads."

Rena seated her guests and passed the food around. Generous helpings were piled on the plates and talk was scarce for a few minutes while everyone savored the delicious food.

"This is the best meal I've had since I came to Socorro," Will said.

"It tastes better than what Suzie and I usually have," Shawn added.

After a while, Rena took the apple pie from the warming oven and covered generous slices with ice cream for dessert. As she refilled the coffee cups, she asked Will, "When are you heading back to Houston?"

"I wish never," Will answered with a grin, "but I should be back in the office by next Tuesday. I'll leave here tomorrow."

Somehow I've got to have a private talk with you, Rena thought.

Suzie and Isabel offered to clear the table and wash the dishes. Rena took her guests into the living room. "Who plays the guitar?" Will asked, seeing the instrument leaning up against the wall.

"It's Rena," Shawn replied. "How about some music, Rena?"

"I'll second that," Will said. "I'd like to hear some of the old songs."

"Like *Strawberry Roan* and *Cowboy Jack*?" Rena asked.

"Yes!" Will said. "And throw in *The Yellow Rose of Texas* and *When the Work's All Done This Fall*."

"Sing with me," Rena said to Will. "You probably know these songs better than I."

"You notice she didn't ask me to sing," Shawn said with a wink.

Suzie and Isabel soon joined them. "Help us sing this old favorite, girls," Rena said as she started the first verse of *You Are My Sunshine*.

They all finished the song with laughs of satisfaction, and Rena got up to put the guitar away. "One more," Will pleaded. "How about Marty Robbins' *El Paso* song?"

"That's so long," Rena said with a sigh, "but I love it."

When Rena ended the ballad some five minutes later, she was amazed at the emotional effect the last verse had on her. As she sang, *From out of nowhere Falina has found me, kissing my cheek as she kneels by my side. Cradled by two loving arms that I'd die for, one little kiss and Falina, goodbye*," she felt the tears sting her eyes. But everyone clapped loudly for her, and she quickly turned her head away and started putting her guitar back in its case. Life can be so sad, she thought.

When the hostess turned back to her guests, she had composed her emotions, and she suddenly had an idea of how she could spend some private time with Will. "I want to send a cake home with you, Shawn. It's a good chocolate cake my neighbor gave me, and I'm not going to eat it. So you and Suzie can enjoy it."

"We sure won't turn that down," Shawn said happily.

"Now, because you are so crowded in your truck, and the cake will just load you down more, why don't I give Will a ride back to town," Rena suggested. She gave Shawn a meaningful look, and he realized instantly her reason for this plan.

"That's fine with us if it's all right with Will," Shawn said.

"I hate to put you out, Lorena, but it certainly would be my pleasure," Will said graciously.

As everyone went out the door, Rena ran back to the far bedroom and hastily stuffed the three yellowed notes in her blouse pocket. "Be with you in a minute," she called, and under her breath added, "There's a reason I want to drive you back to town, Will Estes."

15

RENA WAS NERVOUS as she drove over the rough country lane that led to the main road. "How did you travel to Socorro?" she finally asked, initiating a conversation.

"I drove," Will replied.

"How long does it take you to drive from Houston to Socorro?"

"Most people would make it a two day drive. I make it a long one day drive. I don't stop, except for gas."

"You don't stop for meals?"

"Naw, I just pick up a few snacks when I get gas."

"I suppose you could make good time that way."

The two people then sat in silence for a few miles. It's not an uneasy silence, though, Rena realized. It's almost as if we're old friends.

"Do you like Houston?" Rena finally ventured another question.

"I don't like Houston in the true meaning of the word. But it's where I make a very good living. I work in the city, but I live about fifty miles south in a suburb. It's actually very quiet and peaceful there, almost like living in a small town. It's a little development started by the Quakers many years ago. They created their own little village apart from the rest of the city. Their quiet personality instilled into the area by these original citizens still exists in Friendswood today."

"Nice name," Rena said. "I guess it's a perfect name for a Quaker town."

"It seems to be," Will said.

"Is the Quaker Church still the main church there?"

"As a matter of fact it is. I go there occasionally."

"Do the men sit on one side and the women on the other?"

"No," Will said and smiled. "I think you would find it similar to many other churches. The members are very sincere and spiritual."

As Rena turned off the main highway into Socorro, Will said, "Getting off the subject of Quakers, I have an idea. There's a quiet little tavern in my hotel. Would you like to have a drink with me, and we can visit a while longer, if you're not too tired."

"That would be nice and relaxing," Rena said, and added to herself, I think!

Rena parked in front of the hotel, and Will quickly got out and came around to open the door for her. "It's nice to be with a gentleman," she commented.

They walked through the lobby where a young man at the counter flashed them an artificial smile.

Will then led Rena to a booth at the end of the room away from a talkative group near the bar. A dark-eyed Spanish girl appeared to take their order as soon as they sat down.

"What can I get you?" she asked pleasantly.

Will raised his eyebrows at Rena as he forwarded the question to her. "Rena?"

"I'll have a cherry Coke," she said, smiling. "That's been my favorite drink since I worked in the drug store when I was in high school." To herself, she added, and it will clear my brain for the rest of this conversation.

"You wouldn't have a glass of wine?" Will asked.

"No, thank you," Rena said. "I'm not like my mother that way. She liked her wine."

"I'll have a whiskey and soda," Will said to the waitress.

"This is a nice place," Rena remarked. "I've never been here."

"You haven't had time to take in the night life of Socorro?" Will asked.

"No, I was pretty busy with Mother after I brought her home."

"She was lucky to have a daughter to bring her home and take such good care of her," Will said quietly.

"Well, she did tell me a couple of times I was a good girl. That meant a lot to me because we were never that close as I grew up. I always had the idea she thought I was a terrible daughter." Rena quickly took a drink of Coke as soon as the waitress placed it in front of her.

Will lifted his glass and took a slow sip. Setting it down, he said, "Your mother loved you very much, Rena. I happen to know that."

How do you know it? Rena thought. Aloud, she said, "I was always very close to my father. I knew he loved me."

"Yes, he did. He was very proud of you. He especially bragged about your riding ability," Will said with a smile.

"We always had that love in common," Rena said. "The love of a good horse was probably our most important connection; maybe our other relationships took second place."

"Perhaps so," Will said, nodding.

"Did you find my father difficult to work for?" Rena asked.

"Not really. Mainly, my job was breaking horses. I knew what I was doing, so we got along fine about my work."

"Why did you leave the ranch?" Rena asked as she concentrated on the blue straw she twisted in her drink.

"It was time to move on," Will said. "I had some money saved up, and I decided to go to college. I had bummed around a couple of years on the ranches in the area since I had come home from Korea. I'd done some rodeoing, and I was a very good rider. I considered going professional, but I decided college under the GI Bill was the wiser way to go. I headed south to Texas Tech."

"Have you been happy about your choice?" Rena asked.

"Yes, for the most part. I started going to rodeos as a spectator instead of competing in them. Houston has a huge rodeo every year."

"What else do you do in Houston besides work?" Rena asked.

"I go to Galveston occasionally. I have a beach house and a sail boat that I take out when the Gulf winds are behaving."

Rena took a long drink of her Coke. "That sounds like fun," she said. "What about friends?" she added, trying to sound nonchalant. "Or family? Did you marry in Houston?"

"No," Will responded quietly. "I've never married, but I have many good friends."

Rena pushed her drink aside. Her stomach was starting to churn. It was time to ask some questions about her mother.

"Tell me about my mother. As I said, I was never very close to her, and I never felt as if I knew her very well. Did you get well acquainted with her when you worked on the ranch?"

"Yes, we became very good friends," Will said. "I found her to be a very admirable woman."

"What do you mean?" Rena asked.

"She was a tireless worker," Will replied. "She worked hard in her garden and her vineyard. She cleaned and cooked for hired men and canned food for the winter and made very good wine."

"I know she was a hard worker. But what went on inside her mind? Did you know her well enough to form any opinions?"

"Well, yes." Will hesitated a moment and then added slowly, "I think she had a very good mind. I always thought she should have had some education to give her mind a chance to grow. She married young and moved to the next-door ranch. I frankly thought she felt stifled by the fences around the ranch, even though it was a very large ranch."

This was a new idea to Rena. Had her mother really wished for a broader life?

"Did she have any talents?" Rena asked slowly. "She always seemed impatient with the time my dad and I spent on our music."

"Perhaps she craved a different kind of music. Did you ever think about taking her to a concert in Albuquerque?" Will looked at Rena with thoughtful eyes.

"No," Rena said, obviously surprised at this thought. "I never dreamed of her liking anything like that."

"She loved to dance, too. Did you ever see her dance?" Now it seemed as if Will were interrogating Rena.

"No," Rena replied. "My dad and I played music for dances, but she never went with us." Rena frowned. How does he know she liked to dance? The question seared through her brain, but she didn't have the nerve to pursue it. Instead Rena changed the line of conversation.

"You said I look like my mother. I never thought of myself being anything like my mother, in looks or personality, either one."

Will spoke in a low vibrant voice. "You look very much like your mother, and perhaps you're more like her than you think. Addie was a very sensitive woman. The cold exterior you may have perceived really concealed a vulnerable person who was hurt easily." Will paused and then continued, "Your mother was a beautiful woman, outwardly and inwardly. She was quiet and loyal, and she loved you with all her heart and soul."

"It was my brother she loved with all her heart and soul," Rena said, correcting his statement.

"I didn't know your brother," Will said. "But I know beyond any question what your mother's feelings were for you."

"You seem to have known my mother very well. Wasn't that somewhat unusual between a hired man and the wife of the boss?" The words shot out of Rena's mouth with the quickness of a flying arrow.

Will's direct gaze dropped. At that moment the waitress appeared. "Bring me another," Will said motioning to his glass, and Rena noticed his voice broke a little. "How about you, Lorena?"

"No thanks," she replied, shortly.

When the waitress left, Will looked up again into Rena's inquiring eyes. "Your mother and I became very good friends. I probably needed someone to talk to about my tough army duty, and I think she needed someone to just talk to. She didn't communicate well with most people."

Certainly not her family, Rena thought. "You had a rough time in Korea?" she asked politely.

"Yes, but we aren't here to talk about that," Will said. "Your mother is the only person with whom I ever shared those experiences. She's the only person I ever felt I could talk with about that time of my life."

And she needed someone to understand her, too, Rena thought. One thing led to another, I suppose. She looked over Will's head and watched the bird in the cuckoo clock over the bar bob its head and mark the hour in its unique trilly voice. It's time, she silently told the silly bird. She turned her gaze to Will and asked distinctly, "Were you in love with my mother?"

At that moment the waitress came back with Will's drink. He laid some money on her tray and quickly lifted the glass to his mouth. Then he set the drink down on the table and met Rena's intense gaze. "In all honesty, Rena, I loved your mother very much," he said in a low voice. "The truth of the matter is that I have never felt the same about another woman. I suppose that's why I never married. No one could ever quite take her place. I'm sorry, but that's the truth."

"Is that the real reason you left the ranch?" Rena asked in a tight voice.

"Yes," Will said, dropping his head. "Someone saw Addie and me in our meeting place in the vineyard down by the river and told your father. I knew she wouldn't go with me because I had tried to talk her into that plan before. So to avoid trouble, I left."

"Why wouldn't my mother go with you?" Rena persisted.

"Because she wouldn't take you away from your father. She knew the closeness between the two of you. And she wouldn't leave you with him and go by herself. Put to rest any doubts you may ever have had about your mother not loving you. She would have come with me if it hadn't been for you." Will's voice broke with emotion.

Rena felt her anger draining away and being replaced with compassion as she studied the man across from her. However, her contradictory feelings toward this man who had meant so much to her mother frustrated her. "Don't expect me to feel sorry for you," she said in an accusing voice.

They sat in silence for a few minutes until Will finally said, "I tell you these things to explain the events that happened in your mother's and my lives--not to ask for your pity. But I have lived a lonely life, Rena. When I heard of your father's death, I got in touch with Addie. I wanted her to come to Houston. She wouldn't do it, not because of you this time, but because of her son. She said she would not take him away from his heritage. So she loved her son more than her own personal happiness, as well. You're right about the way she cherished her son."

Rena lifted her head and said in a soft voice, "Life is so sad sometimes. I have come to realize that in the past months. And I suppose none of us has a rose garden."

Will smiled and reached over the table and patted Rena's hand. "We just have to play the cards we're dealt and do the best we can, no matter how hard it is," he said.

"I guess you're right, and I thank you for talking to me. I needed to understand some things. I think I do now." Rena looked deeply into Will's sad blue eyes.

"Thank you for understanding," Will said. "I want you to know I never planned to bother the Steiners anymore, but when I saw you in the café, and you were the image of Addie, I couldn't restrain myself from talking to you."

Rena fought back tears as Will stood up and reached in his shirt pocket for a card. "I'll give you this on the long shot that you might want to contact me someday."

Rena took his business card and thanked him. Then she reached in her pocket for the folded notes. "I haven't known what to do with these," she said as she placed them in his hand. "I'll let you decide."

"I'm going on up to my room," Will said as he got up from his chair. "Thank you for the ride. Good luck, my dear." The notes were clutched in a tight fist as he turned to go.

Rena watched the tall man walk toward the stairs. His step was a little slow. His legs are slightly bowed for a business man, she thought. He's still a cowboy at heart, I think.

Rena's thoughts whirled as she sat at the table by herself. Well, I've got this straightened out. Now I'll call Taylor when I get home and tell him I'm coming back to Albuquerque. It's time to decide what to do about my job and my marriage.

Rena lifted her hands to her face. The card Will had given her was still in her fingers, and she felt it dig into her forehead. She put it down and looked at the gold embossed rectangular piece of paper. His name was printed in bold letters: William B. Estes, Engineer, Kellogg Petroleum Company.

"William B. Estes," Rena whispered. "Does the "B" stand for Boone?"

She knew she would never search further for the answer to that question, nor would she ever reveal her suspicions to Boone or to Will.

As Rena drove slowly back to the ranch, she dodged the flitting forms of jack rabbits and concentrated on the unfamiliar picture Will Estes had painted of her mother. He had described her as a woman with a very good mind who should have had some education to realize her potential. She must have craved more than her life here had encompassed. Did she wonder about the world beyond the ranch as Will had said? He had obviously taken her to a concert, and he said her mother loved to dance. She had never known these things about her mother.

Rena's mind went back to the sights and sensations of long ago when she was a child on the ranch. The first sounds and smells that she was aware of in the morning were those of her mother bustling around the kitchen cooking the morning meal. But she knew Addie had been up long before that, doing her chores: milking the cow, gathering the eggs, and checking her wine barrels. Her small sunbonnetted form walked briskly from house to garden to wine cellar all day. She seldom spoke, and her days were perpetual movement. I guess I never thought of her as a person, Rena thought. She was more like a machine. Was she, under her weathered layers of brown skin and behind those cold eyes, the sensitive woman Will described?

Tears came suddenly to Rena's eyes. What a lonely person she might have been. She must have lived in her own world, and no one took the time or interest to try to join her there. "Nobody, except perhaps Billy Estes." Her anguished words filled the car as sobs shook her body, and she cried for the hurt both her father and mother must have suffered.

Rena brushed her eyes with the back of her hand and tried to gulp down her heartbreak. How insensitive I've been all my life, she realized. And I was probably as insensitive with Taylor, too. No wonder I couldn't have a successful marital relationship. Forgive me, Mother. Forgive me, Taylor.

As Rena brushed more tears from her eyes, she suddenly noticed a bright glowing light ahead. "My God!" she said softly. "There's a fire in the bosque."

The real fear of fire consumed Rena's consciousness. Fire was the dreaded word in the woodlands along the river. The dry leaves and dead limbs and brush furnished hot fodder for the flames to lick and spread. Every rancher with land near the bosque lived in constant fear of the possibility of flames destroying his pastures and everything in its path. It happened all too often.

"Suzie's horse." Rena said as she put her foot down hard on the accelerator.

The Buick lurched into the yard, and Rena dashed to the shed to get a halter. There was smoke in the air, and she could hear the crackling of the flames. She grabbed a handful of grain pellets from a bag as she went out the door.

Rena could make out moving figures and vehicles as she ran toward the flames. They are fighting it already, she thought with a feeling of relief. But she could see the fire had already spread practically the whole length of their riverfront land.

As her eyes adjusted to the agitated scene, Rena saw the shadowy form of a horse running toward her. "Come Buck," she called urgently as she held out her hand filled with pellets. She hoped the pellets would distract him from his fear.

The animal circled the woman nervously as she talked softly and steadily to him. "Come on, boy. Come on. It's all right, Buck."

The frightened animal came close enough for Rena to slip the halter around his neck, and she held him firmly and patted his neck reassuringly as he chewed the pellets. "Good boy!" she said as she led him away from the besieged pasture.

Rena quickly put the horse into a holding pen behind Boone's house. She carefully locked the gate and turned to run back to the fire. At that moment, Darlene came out of the house.

"What happened?" Rena asked.

"It flared up just after dark," Darlene replied. "The county fire department seems to be getting it under control."

"But it's burned the whole river shoreline," Rena said anxiously. "And I'm afraid the vineyard is gone."

"But not the whole pasture," Darlene said. "And there's no danger to our houses. They have it contained."

Darlene's steady voice had a calming effect on Rena's nerves. "Are you sure?" she asked, needing more assurance.

"Don't worry," Darlene insisted.

Rena muttered a muted, "Thanks," and hurried toward the bosque. I guess she's more used to this kind of crisis than I, she told herself. She probably knows what she's talking about.

Rena stopped in the middle of the pasture and stood watching the frenzied efforts to quell the fire. Streams of water poured on the flames from the big county fire truck. Several men were beating the flames with shovels and others were digging a fire barrier. Red tongues of fire leaped skyward as they climbed up the big cottonwood trees.

Rena thought sadly of the bosque's beauty. She had often walked along the path that wound in and out of the thick trees and brush as she searched the river surface for ducks and other waterfowl that swam in the quiet eddies along the river edges. She had looked for birds flitting from the thick tree branches and had sometimes flushed out surprised rabbits and road runners in the brush. Skinny little lizards had darted swiftly in and out of the vegetation looking for bugs. The bosque had been so alive; now everything was gone.

A figure separated itself from the smoke and haze and stood in front of Rena. It was Boone with a shovel over his shoulder. "Nothing to worry about," he said loudly. "We got it under control. It took the vineyard, but the wine making days of the ranch have long been over."

"Everything looks terrible," Rena said sadly. "All the lush green beauty has turned into blackened ashes."

"Yeah, a careless campfire does a lot o' damage," Boone said nodding his head. "But this desecration won't last. It won't be a month before the grass will be shootin' up through the ashes. Mother Nature will reclaim her land. And it'll be prettier and greener than ever. A fire actually has a positive effect on the growth that comes later. It won't be stifled by dead grass and brush. The slate is wiped clean for a new beginning for the bosque."

Rena liked the sound of those words, "a new beginning." "Maybe that's what I need," she murmured.

Boone didn't hear her remark. "Go on back home and crawl into bed," he advised. "The men will be here mopping up all night. I see you got the horse. That's fine. She'll be easier out of here for a few days." Boone then gave his sister a pat on her arm and turned to rejoin the fire crew.

Rena stood for a few moments thinking about what had happened in the last few hours. As she watched the flames, a picture suddenly came to her mind. She was twelve years old and her Lutheran confirmation teacher stood before her saying, "Fire is a symbol of the presence of God in the Bible."

Strange how I remember that, she thought. Maybe this is His way of purging this area and purifying it. She was aware of a sense of consolation as she realized that the meeting place of Addie and Will had been burned and totally destroyed. That was good. Maybe all the frustration and wrongness of that relationship went up with the flames and the smoke. Maybe this fire signifies a new beginning for all of us, she thought. Rena felt the bitterness in her life lifting and wafting up toward the vanishing clouds of smoke.

16 ~~~~~~

RENA FELL ONTO HER BED, physically and emotionally exhausted. But she was aware of a strange peace engulfing her as she drifted off into sleep. Finally she knew she had grasped the essence of the woman who had eluded her for so many years. "And you did love me, Mother," she whispered to the stillness of the night.

The next morning Rena hopped out of bed and pulled on a robe while she glanced at the clock beside her bed. "Ten o'clock! How could I have slept so long?" she wondered aloud as the phone's insistent ringing broke into her thoughts.

Shawn's voice greeted her with a cheery, "Good mornin'! Did I wake you up?"

"I just got up," Rena said truthfully. "I really don't know why I slept so long."

"You had too much excitement last night. I hear you had a fire in the bosque."

Rena glanced out the kitchen window toward the river. Smoke still lingered over the treetops. "Yes, but it looks pretty quiet this morning. It was going full force when I came home after leaving Will in town."

"How late did the handsome Mr. Estes keep you up last night?" Shawn said teasingly.

"We visited about an hour, I guess," Rena replied. "I had a Coke with him at the hotel. He did have some interesting memories of my folks."

"That's nice," Shawn said. "Did he leave today? I didn't see him in the café."

"Yes, he's gone," Rena said with finality.

"And what are your plans today?" Shawn asked.

Thinking of her decision the night before, Rena said, "I think I'll go to Albuquerque today. I've got some things I have to do there, so I won't be able to work with Suzie. In fact, I don't know when I can work with her again."

There was a moment's silence on the other end of the line. "Well, could you have lunch with me before you leave?"

"Of course," Rena replied. "I'll meet you at the café at noon."

"That sounds good to me. I'll see you then."

Rena immediately rang her home number in Albuquerque after her conversation with Shawn. She let it ring several times, but there was no answer. So he isn't there, she thought. Well I'm going to Albuquerque anyway.

After a leisurely shower, Rena sat at the kitchen table drinking her coffee. She looked through the kitchen window at the clear sunshiny day which erased the pictures of the fiery night. The familiar sights of the cottonwoods' shimmering yellow leaves framing Suzie's horse as he looked placidly over the fence near Boone's house gave her a feeling of reassurance. She didn't know where today would take her, but she knew she was ready to confront her life. My motor's been running in neutral for months, she told herself. I'm ready to start going forward now.

Her mother's words came back to her mind. "Don't make the same mistake I made." I won't, Mother. I'm going back to Taylor and see if we can make things right with our marriage.

Rena packed her clothes and put them in the Buick. Then she walked over to Boone's house to tell them her plans. Darlene was in the kitchen, the baby was asleep, the girls were quietly playing with their dolls, and Boone was gone. "Did you lose your helper?" Rena asked.

"Yes, he's gone thankfully back to his ranch work," Darlene said with a smile. "He's glad to get out of the house."

"I'm sure," Rena agreed. "Being a housekeeper and nurse and baby sitter wasn't exactly his cup of tea. But he did the best he could. He's a good husband."

"Yes he is," Darlene said with a soft laugh.

"I can't stay," Rena said as Darlene motioned her to a chair. "I just wanted to let you know I'm heading to Albuquerque this morning. I need to talk to Taylor. We've got to get some things straightened out."

"I understand," Darlene said with a knowing look. "What do you think you're going to do?"

"I don't know right now. But I'll figure it out soon."

Rena was headed for the door, as the two girls intercepted her and clung to her legs. "Don't go, Aunt Rena," Merla said tearfully.

"You don't go," Marla reinforced strongly.

Rena suddenly felt uncertainty rushing over her resolve to leave. She knelt and hugged the children who had become so dear to her. Fighting tears, she said, "I have to go for a while, but I'll come back to see you both. You can have fun in the playhouse while I'm gone."

Gently she loosened the tight little arms that held her and hurried out the door. "You tum back soon," Marla called after her receding figure.

Rena honked the horn as she pulled out of the yard. "Goodbye little girls, goodbye ranch. I don't know when I'll be back, or if I'll be back" she said with a pang in her heart.

Shawn was waiting for Rena on the sidewalk in front of the café as she pulled up. He quickly walked to her car and opened the door for her. "That's service," she said with a smile.

"Anything for you, darlin'," he said, favoring her with his dimpled grin.

Shawn led Rena to a booth at the back of the café. As she sat down in the soft seat, a thought seared through her mind. This would be the last time she'd be here with Shawn, and she knew she would miss him.

"So you're heading back to Albuquerque?" Shawn said, attempting light conversation, but his serious brown eyes looked steadily and questioningly at her.

"Yes, Shawn," Rena said, answering his question and his look. "Now that Mother is gone, I've got to put some effort into getting my life back on track."

"Does that mean you're going back to Taylor?" Shawn asked, unable to conceal the anxiety in his voice.

"Maybe," Rena said carefully, "if he wants me."

"I can't imagine anyone not wanting you," Shawn said with a hint of anger.

At that moment the waitress came to their table, and the conversation was interrupted while they ordered. "I'd recommend the special," Shawn said. "The Reuben sandwich and soup are excellent."

"If it's vegetable soup," Rena said. The waitress nodded and smiled and went away, writing their order on a pad.

Shawn then changed the subject to Suzie. He wanted Rena's opinion about her riding progress. Rena assured him she had done very well. All she had to do was keep riding as often as possible, and she should be in good shape to compete in the "Miss Rodeo" contest the next summer. "I'll try to come back and help her with her clothes. She'll need to choose the right kind of western suits," Rena told Shawn.

"That would be a big help to us," Shawn said.

"And I'll teach her the queen wave as she gallops at top speed around the arena," Rena said with a smile.

"I'm sure that's very important," Shawn said wryly.

"Very!" Rena said, widening her eyes.

"If you decide to come back, there'll be other girls who will want you to help them," Shawn said. "Heck, you could start your own riding school."

"I would love that," Rena said. "Talk about doing the work you love! That would be it for me."

"What are you going to do about your job?" Shawn asked tentatively.

"I'll keep it if I stay in Albuquerque," Rena answered.

At that moment their lunch arrived, and they ate in silence for a while. Finally Shawn said quietly, "It's been nice having you here."

Rena looked up from her soup. "I want to thank you for all your support, Shawn. You've been there for me as you always were in the past. You are a good friend."

"I'll always be there for you, Lorena. If you need anything, just call me. I'm only an hour and a half away, you know."

"Thanks Shawn," Rena said with sincerity.

Shawn stood on the street as Rena backed her car out and headed for

Albuquerque. She could see him in her rear view mirror when she headed north. He raised his hand in a goodbye salute. He's a special person, she thought. He deserves the best, not a battered failure like me.

As Rena sped down the highway, her thoughts went back to her conversation with Will Estes. He obviously knew Mother a lot better than I did, she thought. And better than Dad did, too.

Rena knew her mother had been very young when she married her father. Maybe she grew in one way and he in another as the years went by, she reasoned. That happens. I should know.

As she analyzed Will Estes, she found her resentment abating. I guess he truly loved her, and she must have loved him. But because of Boone and me, she didn't leave Daddy. What a lonely, unhappy life she must have had. Maybe that's what made her seem so cold and uncaring.

Poor Daddy. He knew about Will's and Mother's feelings for each other. Is that why he resorted to the bottle to soothe his heartbreak? Is that why he stayed away from home so much and visited the night spots in Magdalena so regularly? He must have gone through hell. Dear God, what people put each other through in this world.

Rena's thoughts raced on. Mother never trusted me after I became a teenager. Lord knows, I was very boy crazy. Because she had been tempted in her marriage, did she worry I would use poor judgment in my personal life? Is that why she was so hard on me? She told me not to make the same mistake she made. She didn't want me to become interested in another man besides my husband.

Well, Mother, I'm going back to Albuquerque and see if I can make things right with Taylor. I owe that to him. Rena shook her head sadly as her thoughts continued. Heaven knows I haven't been a good wife. I did make the same mistake my mother made. Apparently I am my mother's daughter. But I hope it isn't too late to mend things. I've got to try.

Taylor's car was parked in front of the house. "Good, he's here," Rena said with resoluteness as she drove into the driveway of her Albuquerque home. She took a deep breath and walked briskly up the sidewalk to the front door.

17

THE DOOR HANDLE TURNED EASILY, and Rena moved quietly into the living room of her home. A feeling of security swept over her as she looked around at the familiar furniture and pictures and pottery. She paused at the hand-woven wall hanging she had bought in Santa Fe and ran her fingers over the silver ponies that galloped down the center of it. "So pretty," she said softly. She had loved decorating her home.

Knowing Taylor must be here somewhere, Rena headed for the kitchen. A package of chips, a loaf of bread, a jar of mayonnaise, and two small plates were on the table. She automatically put the mayonnaise jar in the refrigerator and glanced through the kitchen window to the patio. She could see Taylor stretched out on a lounge chair talking to someone she couldn't see. The happiness she had felt upon coming into her home was suddenly replaced with trepidation. Go on out there and talk to him, she told herself.

Rena went through the screen door and looked toward the chair where she had seen Taylor. He was lifting his glass to take a drink, and when he realized who had just appeared, he held it suspended in midair. Rena's eyes took in the whole scene, which included a woman sitting in a recliner next to the door, looking up at her with startled eyes.

"Well, hello!" Rena said in a voice that was surprisingly calm.

Taylor quickly jumped up and set his glass down on the patio table. "You should have called me you were coming," he said in a protesting voice.

"Obviously," Rena said sweetly as her gaze met the agitated eyes of the other woman.

Taylor reached a hand out to help his companion up and began a nervous introduction. "Rena, this is Carol, a friend."

"I'm Rena Brooks, his wife," Rena said, finishing the introduction, with emphasis on the word, "wife." She took the limp hand and looked straight into the furtive light brown eyes of Taylor's friend, Carol. She looks like a scared bird ready to flutter her wings and fly away, Rena thought.

"Sit down," Taylor said hastily, pulling up a chair.

Rena sat down calmly. I can't believe how much in control I feel, she thought. "I tried to call you this morning, Taylor."

"I was out for a while this morning," Taylor said quickly.

There was a moment's silence. "I thought we should talk," Rena finally said.

"That's right," Taylor replied in a voice that was a little too loud. "We do have some things to discuss."

Rena looked at the woman. She had said nothing yet. Both she and Taylor had been talking as if Carol wasn't there. "I'm sorry if I have interrupted your visit, Carol."

The woman swallowed visibly. "It's all right," she said in a low voice. Her lashes moved swiftly up and down over eyes which were beseeching Taylor's help.

He rose with some of his old assurance. Giving Rena a disdainful look, he said, "I'll take Carol home. Then we can talk."

Rena leaned back in her chair and found herself chuckling as they went into the house. I have actually been through "the other woman" scene, she thought. And I'm laughing about it. She's such a hopeless creature. Couldn't he have found someone better than that to replace me?

But suddenly the laughter turned to tears. What about the one you were seeing? she reminded herself. Older, receding hairline, not exactly Clark Gable. All he really had going for himself were his money and his Chief of Staff title. "And that impressed me," Rena said disgustedly as she swept her hand over her eyes in irritation.

Rena stood up. She knew Taylor wouldn't be back for a while. He would have to reassure his trembling little bird. I'll go to the hospital, she decided, and I'll talk to my boss about submitting my resignation. Now she knew she probably wouldn't be staying in Albuquerque.

Rena parked her car at the hospital and hurried with sure steps into the waiting room. "Hello Regina," she greeted the receptionist. "Is Paula in her office?"

Regina looked at Rena with a smile. "You're back! It's good to see you, and yes, I'll let Paula know you're here."

Paula came out of her office and swept Rena into a tight hug. "I'm so glad to see you," she said as she stepped back, looking into Rena's eyes. "I'm so sorry about your mother." Again Rena was embraced by loving arms. The two were friends as well as professional colleagues.

The women then headed into Paula's office and sat down. Rena took out a handkerchief and wiped her eyes. "It's good to see you, Paula," she said with a wane smile.

"How are you doing?" Paula asked with genuine compassion. "I know you've been through a bad time."

"I'm doing fine," Rena said as she lifted her chin and put the hankie away. "In fact, I'm going to be doing better from now on."

"What are you going to do?" Paula asked cautiously. "I hope this doesn't mean you're leaving us."

"I'm afraid so," Rena said. "I'm going back home, Paula. Back to the ranch. That's where I feel I belong now."

"I understand," Paula said, "but I'll miss you."

"Thanks for being so good to me all these years," Rena said. "You've been one wonderful boss lady."

"You did a good job and were a valuable employee," Paula said simply.

"Well," Rena said as she stood up, "do you think I could give my notice today instead of waiting two weeks? I'd like to clean out my desk."

Paula rose and said with a smile, "Of course you can. I hired a woman as a temp employee for three months when you left. She'll be happy to know I'm keeping her on."

"Thank you so much," Rena said as she embraced Paula again and headed for her old office.

The name on the door was a strange one to her, and when she walked in and saw someone else at her desk, she experienced a momentarily unsettling feeling. Don't waver, she instructed herself.

To the questioning face behind the desk, she said, "I'm Rena Brooks. I'd like to borrow my old office for a few minutes. I need to write a letter of resignation."

The woman looked at her with wide eyes and then smiled broadly. "Of course," she said as she headed for the door. "I'll go down to the cafeteria for a break. Stay as long as you wish."

"Be back in fifteen minutes," Rena called after her. "It won't take me long."

After Rena finished her letter, she opened the desk drawer. She remembered that she had thrown her wedding rings in there the day she had decided to take her mother home to the ranch. Where are they? She wondered. She didn't see them. "Where are they?" she said aloud just as her replacement walked back in the room.

"Where is what?" the woman asked.

"I left some rings in here," Rena said anxiously. "I don't see them."

"Here they are," the woman said as she stepped behind the desk and opened a paper clip box. "You left them just lying in the drawer, and I thought they would be a little safer in a box."

"Thank you for taking care of them," Rena said graciously as she started for the door. "Good luck with your job." She put the rings in the coin holder in her purse and zipped them up with finality.

Rena walked back down the hall and left her letter of resignation with Regina. As she headed for her car, she felt as if she were walking on clouds. "I'm free," she exulted. "I'm free!" She had given that hospital many of the best years of her life.

Well, not exactly, she corrected herself as she headed east on Lomas Street back to her home. I really need to make amends with my husband if at all possible. Maybe I should give it one more try.

Taylor was sitting in the living room when Rena walked in. His face was set in a confrontational mode. "You're alone now?" Rena asked, trying to keep the sarcasm out of her voice.

"I'm alone," Taylor said stiffly.

"Carol is your secretary, right?" Rena asked. Might as well get to the point, she thought.

"Yes," Taylor replied quietly. "She was my secretary. We work in different departments now."

And that is the plain little wren that turned my life upside down, Rena thought. I can't believe it. She looked at Taylor's drawn face and suddenly felt sorry for him.

"I came back, Taylor, to try to salvage our marriage. We did make vows to each other, and maybe we should endeavor to keep some of them, even though some have been broken." There was no bitterness in her voice. She knew he was no more guilty than she.

"Maybe the marriage isn't salvageable," Taylor said in a low voice.

Rena looked at Taylor's downcast face in surprise. He's really a good man at heart, she admitted to herself. He just married the wrong woman.

"Perhaps you're right," she said. "Taylor, we haven't had a real marriage for a long time. It's not all your fault. It started with me when I enticed you into marrying me so I could get away from home. You know we never had the deep love and dedication for each other that's needed to build a life-time relationship. So we both looked around for other people. Each one of us is guilty."

Taylor gazed at Rena with disbelieving eyes. He was astonished at her words. He had expected her to be raving in anger at him. He opened his mouth, but no words came out.

"I came back to see if we could somehow fix this ailing marriage of ours. Maybe as you say, that isn't possible. Do you love her, Taylor? Do you love Carol?"

"Yes," Taylor managed to say in a weak voice.

Rena suddenly felt compassion for Taylor. He had been her husband and had worked hard for them. But the marriage had never been right. "I'm tired and hungry, Taylor," Rena said as she stood up. Could we go to some quiet place for dinner? We've got some decisions to make."

"Sure, there's a new place down on Indian School Road. We can go there." For the first time since Rena had walked in the door, there was relief on Taylor's face and in his voice.

"Let me make a stop in the bathroom and wash my hands. I'll be right back," Rena said as she headed down the hall.

Yes, she thought ironically, it's time to wash this marriage right out of my hands.

18 ~~~~~~

LATER, SITTING ALONE IN THE PATIO of her Albuquerque home, Rena went back over the evening's events. She smiled as she remembered that Taylor had eaten very little of the dinner he had ordered; she had enjoyed her steak with gusto.

The conversation regarding the divorce had been short and to the point. She had said, "You want a divorce; I want one, too. Let's get started on it immediately. I have a lawyer in Socorro, and I would prefer to file for the divorce."

Taylor had concurred, and it had taken very little time for them to reach agreement on the property settlement. The house would be sold, and the proceeds divided equally. She would take the Buick, and he would take the Lincoln. Their investments would be sold and the money divided equally.

"I don't really need any of it," Rena had said lightly. "I'm a ranch owner now."

"Are you going to live there?" Taylor had asked, curiosity in his voice.

"Yes," Rena had said. "I'm ready to go home, Taylor. Albuquerque was never really home to me. It's just where I lived and worked. We never made our house a home. Don't you agree?"

Taylor had nodded. "I'm afraid you're right. I'm sorry, Rena. I really am." Then he had asked if she planned to work in Socorro.

Rena remembered thinking that he was trying to pretend to be interested in her future. Aloud she had said, "I think I'll build some barns

~~~~~~ **127**

and corrals and have a horse business. I'd like to train barrel horses and give riding lessons. I've been working with a young girl, and I've discovered I really have a passion for this kind of work."

"You always liked your horses," Taylor had said with a sigh.

"And you never understood my interest in them," Rena had said flatly.

He had then changed the subject by inviting her to stay in the house that night and pack whatever she wanted to take.

I could have asked for anything, and he'd have given it to me, Rena had told herself. He just wants this over as soon as possible, which suits me fine. Aloud, she'd said, "I'll make a call tonight to get a pickup over here. I should be out of the house by tomorrow afternoon and I'll leave the key under the mat."

It had been a silent ride back to the house after dinner. Rena had looked out her window as the houses sped by. I came here to repair my marriage, she had thought. Instead, it's being totally dissolved.

Then her thoughts had turned to her mother. I tried to straighten it out, Mother, she had silently pleaded. But it just won't work. She had put her head down and raised her hand to cover her eyes from Taylor's view.

In the silence of her struggling thoughts, realization had suddenly cut swiftly through the chaos. She told me not to make the same mistake she made. Maybe she wasn't talking about the affair with Will. Maybe she didn't regret that. Could her mistake have been in deciding to remain tied to a loveless marriage rather than going with the man she loved? Could that have been the mistake her mother was thinking about?

Rena had put her hand down and opened her eyes wide as she looked out the car window. The last bright rays of the southwestern sun were dancing off the stucco homes in splurges of brilliance before fading away behind the western hills. Her mind was suddenly crystal clear. That's it! she had told herself with elation. That's really what she was trying to tell me! She couldn't come right out and plainly tell me she had made a mistake staying with my father.

When Taylor had pulled into the yard and stopped the car, he'd hurried around to open the door for Rena. As she stepped out, she had given him a wide smile. "Thank you, Taylor. Thank you and goodbye. I hope you'll remember me a little fondly." You had to add that sarcastic little remark, Lorena chastised herself with a grin.

Taylor had silently headed back to the driver's side of his car.

"Wait," Rena had called as she suddenly remembered the rings. She had unzipped her purse and felt in the change compartment for them. She had taken them out and walked to Taylor. "You can have these. I don't need them," she had said as she put them in his outstretched hand. He had looked at them blankly for a second and then closed his fingers and turned away.

His methodical mind didn't compute my actions and words, Rena thought with amusement. But he'll understand the money he gets for the rings when he sells them or trades them in on a set for Carol.

As the day's events continued to roll chaotically through Rena's mind in disorderly flashbacks, she rested an arm over weary eyes. Taylor's face appeared, filled with consternation and impatience. That's the way he looked when I appeared on the patio and found him with Carol, she thought with a grimace. "Too bad I upset the convenient little playhouse he has so carefully contrived. He must have thought I was pretty stupid," she said out loud. She shook her head in disgust. "Well, Carol" she said with a final sigh, "you can have him and my second-hand rings."

Rena pulled absent-mindedly on her ring finger and then opened her eyes as she held her hand above her head. "Rings all gone," she whispered, and when the tears threatened to come, she admonished herself, "No more tears, Lorena. Do you hear me? No more tears!"

Rena blinked in surprise as a bright flash of light suddenly sped through the darkness of the night, headed straight for Rena's face. Before her astonished eyes, the moving light paused momentarily before making a quick flip and heading back into obscurity. Rena gasped at the unexpected confrontation and then smiled as she realized she had been in the path of a firefly's journey.

"I haven't seen a firefly in ages!" she exclaimed. As the tiny speck of light faded away, she murmured, "He just had to make a detour on the path he was traveling. In fact, he made an about-face and turned himself completely around."

Rena sat up straight on her patio lounger. She noticed the moon starting to appear over the mountains to the east. Her eyes remained riveted on the plump golden ball that quickly rose in its entirety to rule the darkness of the night. Rena gazed at it in hypnotized fascination. First the firefly, she thought, now the moon. Both of them moving on without hesitation. Are they trying to tell me something?

Rena stood up, squared her shoulders, smiled wryly at the moon, and walked into the house with purposeful steps. She picked up the telephone, realizing she was about to make her first move toward a new beginning. "Shawn said if I needed help to give him a call," she reminded herself.

"Hello." Suzie's bright voice trilled over the line.

"Hi Suz, it's me!" Rena said, feeling her spirits lift at the sound of the girl's voice.

"Oh Rena! I'm so glad to hear from you. When are you coming back? We miss you."

Rena swallowed hard, realizing she was hearing from the world where she belonged. "I plan to be home soon, dear," she said quickly. "Can I talk to your father?"

Shawn's voice came over the miles with steady strength. "Hello Rena. Glad to hear from you. How are things going?"

Rena visualized his concerned brown eyes. "I'm fine," she said in a reassuring voice. "Taylor and I had a good talk tonight. We agree on everything, the divorce and the settlement."

"I'm sorry, Rena," Shawn said quietly.

"I'm sorry, too, but I'm happy. Shawn, I need someone with a pickup to haul my things out of this house. I could call Boone if it's any trouble."

"I can do that," Shawn said with enthusiasm in his voice. "No trouble at all, I assure you. I can come up tonight or in the morning."

"Tomorrow morning would be fine. I'll pack tonight."

"I'll be there by seven o'clock. Have breakfast ready for me, and then we'll load up. How does that sound?"

"Wonderful!"

"By the way, a woman who is establishing a school for children with special needs approached me today. She thinks riding lessons would be good therapy for her students, and she's interested in hiring a riding teacher. I didn't tell her about you because I didn't know if you'd be coming back."

"I'd love that," Rena said happily. All the pieces of her complicated life suddenly seemed to be falling into place.

"Well, you're good with kids. Suzie and I know that for sure, and we'll vouch for you." Shawn said. "You can talk with her when you get back here."

"Thank you so much, Shawn. You're the best. I'll see you in the morning."

"Yeah, I'm looking forward to that," Shawn replied, and then added in a soft voice, "And Rena, I'm so glad you're coming home."

After she gently hung up the phone, Rena said out loud. "I've got to get my packing done." She walked past the picture window and glanced at the moon, which seemed to be beaming down its approval. With a satisfied smile, she thought, yes, I'm going back to the land and my roots. Back to security. Back to family and the innocent laughter of two dark eyed little girls. Back to work, and a new challenge, and a new life. Back to honesty and decency. Back to self-respect and maybe even love . . . someday. Thank you, God. Thank you . . . Mother.

$18.34 2011
New

Printed in the United States
45286LVS00007B/415-486